Jenny shivered
all the way down her spine.

She told herself it was because of the cold wind that blew into the kitchen in the quick second before Zach turned to close the door. But it wasn't.

The cold had turned the man into someone who looked as if he belonged on one of those calendars. He was Mr. December.

Just look at him, she thought in dismay. She wasn't supposed to meet a man like Zach, whose face would make a nun shiver. But there he stood against the black of the night like some mountain man, covered with snow.

D0724799

Dear Reader,

Grab a front-row seat on the roller-coaster ride of falling in love. This month, Silhouette Romance offers heart-spinning thrills, including the latest must-read from THE COLTONS saga, a new enchanting SOULMATES title and even a sexy Santa!

Become a fan—if you aren't hooked already!—of THE COLTONS with the newest addition to the legendary family saga, Teresa Southwick's *Sky Full of Promise* (#1624), about a stone-hearted doctor in search of a temporary fiancée. And single men don't stay so for long in Jodi O'Donnell's BRIDGEWATER BACHELORS series. The next rugged Texan loses his solo status in *His Best Friend's Bride* (#1625).

Love is magical, and it's especially true in our wonderful SOULMATES series, which brings couples together in extraordinary ways. In DeAnna Talcott's *Her Last Chance* (#1628), virgin heiress Mallory Chevalle travels thousands of miles in search of a mythical horse—and finds her destiny in the arms of a stubborn, but irresistible rancher. And a case of amnesia reunites past lovers—but the heroine's painful secret could destroy her second chance at happiness, in Valerie Parv's *The Baron & the Bodyguard*, the latest exciting installment in THE CARRAMER LEGACY.

To get into the holiday spirit, enjoy Janet Tronstad's *Stranded with Santa* (#1626), a fun-loving romp about a rodeo megastar who gets stormbound with a beautiful young widow. Then, discover how to melt a Scrooge's heart in Moyra Tarling's *Christmas Due Date* (#1629)

I hope you enjoy these stories, and please keep in touch!

Mary-Theresa Hussey

Mary-Theresa Hussey
Senior Editor

Please address questions and book requests to:
Silhouette Reader Service
U.S.: 3010 Walden Ave., P.O. Box 1325, Buffalo, NY 14269
Canadian: P.O. Box 609, Fort Erie, Ont. L2A 5X3

Stranded
with Santa

JANET TRONSTAD

SILHOUETTE *Romance*®

Published by Silhouette Books

America's Publisher of Contemporary Romance

This book is dedicated to my good friend,
Darlene Hanson,
and her mother,
Pearl Hanson

SILHOUETTE BOOKS

ISBN 0-373-19626-1

STRANDED WITH SANTA

Copyright © 2002 by Janet Tronstad

This edition published by arrangement with Harlequin Books S.A.

® and TM are trademarks of Harlequin Books S.A., used under license.
Trademarks indicated with ® are registered in the United States Patent
and Trademark Office, the Canadian Trade Marks Office and in other
countries.

Visit Silhouette at www.eHarlequin.com

Printed in U.S.A.

Books by Janet Tronstad

Silhouette Romance

Stranded with Santa #1626

Steeple Hill Love Inspired

*An Angel for Dry Creek #81
*A Gentleman for Dry Creek #110
*A Bride for Dry Creek #138
*A Rich Man for Dry Creek #176

*Dry Creek

JANET TRONSTAD

grew up on a small farm in central Montana. One of her favorite things to do was to visit her grandfather's bookshelves, where he had a large collection of Zane Grey novels. She's always loved a good story.

Today, Janet lives in Pasadena, California, where she works in the research department of a medical organization. In addition to writing novels, she researches and writes nonfiction magazine articles.

Dear Santa,

I've been a good boy all year.

The reason I'm writing is to let you know we moved after my dad died. We're in Montana now. Me and my sister like it here. There's bugs all over and rabbits and snakes. My mom is scared of the snakes.

That's why I need a cowboy outfit for Christmas, like the kind Zach "Lightning" Lucas wears. If I had one, I could rope some rabbits and shoot the snakes so my mom wouldn't be scared.

I know about money and how there's not much around, so if a cowboy outfit is too expensive maybe you could send a real cowboy instead. Then my mom wouldn't be scared of nothing.

Thanks,
Andy Collins

P.S. My sister wants one of those princess crowns with jewels on it.

Chapter One

Zach Lucas stood on a weathered old porch in the small town of Deep Gulch, Montana, and scowled as the gray sky darkened even further. "It's going to snow."

Dr. Norris, the only vet in Deep Gulch, Montana, shrugged as he cheerfully slipped another handful of candy canes into the mail bag Zach had slung over his shoulder. "Don't worry about the snow. The postal truck always makes it through. You'll do fine."

The doctor had made a bargain with Zach. It was Saturday, December 23, and Zach was to deliver the mail along the rural route outside of Deep Gulch so that the doctor, who had promised he would do his sister's mail route in her absence, could tend to Zach's sick horse instead.

It was a perfect bargain except for one small thing. Zach hated it.

If he wasn't so worried about his horse, Zach would never have agreed. It wasn't that he had anything against delivering the mail. That was no problem. What was a problem was delivering it the way the doctor's sister wanted it done. She wanted it to look like Santa himself was out there delivering the letters this close to Christmas.

Zach pushed his Stetson hat lower on his head. He didn't know anyone in this crazy one-stop town, but he still hoped no one saw him as he stood on the doctor's porch. He was Zach "Lightning" Lucas and he had a reputation to uphold—a reputation that didn't include a fuzzy red fat-suit and a plastic black belt. It was bad enough that the four-wheel-drive postal truck had a fake set of reindeer horns tied to the grill and a ball of mistletoe swinging from the antenna. He didn't need Christmas fuzz all over him, too.

Zach grimaced as red and green flashes met his eyes. The lightbulbs hanging from the reindeer horns were on a timer. When he first saw them, he'd hoped they were merely ornamental. No such luck.

Zach didn't know how much holiday nonsense he could take. After all, he was Zach "Lightning" Lucas. He had more gold-plated champion belt buckles than most men had ties. He had fans who knew his name—lots of fans since he'd endorsed that Ranger breakfast cereal. People recognized him in grocery stores and in laundromats. He was famous, for Pete's sake. He was entitled to some dignity.

Unfortunately, the doctor did not care about Zach's dignity.

And it was all because of Christmas. Not that Zach should be surprised. Christmas had been giving him trouble for years. It always depressed him with all that family stuff. Not that Zach had anything against families—it's just that that family stuff wasn't for a man like him.

That's why, this year, he had made a plan.

Zach and Thunder were only passing through Montana, heading over to Interstate 15 for the long stretch down to Las Vegas. Once there, Thunder would board at a ranch some miles outside of Vegas while Zach hit the Strip. The neon lights and showgirls—well, if her return message was to be believed, one showgirl in particular—would make him forget the holidays were even here.

He and Thunder had been making good time, too, Zach thought mournfully, until Thunder got a fever.

"You've got the map." The older man patted his pockets as though the slip of paper showing all the county roads might still be there instead of taped to the dashboard of the postal truck.

"Yes, sir."

The winter air had a bite to it, but Zach was in no hurry to leave the doctor's porch and get into that decked-out postal truck. He might as well ride around in a clown's cart and be done with it.

"Well then, let me get that apple pie my sister baked for the Collins family." Dr. Norris ducked inside his house, his muffled voice continuing, "That'll be the last stop on your list. And the box in back is for them, too. Their car is broken. Radiator. So Delores said she'd pick some things up for them." The doctor appeared again with a foil-wrapped pie. "Two of the cutest kids you'll ever meet."

Zach nodded. He'd already met every kid on the planet—both the cute and the ugly. The ones he missed at the rodeos he met because they ate Ranger breakfast cereal. Not that he was complaining. He liked kids better than he liked most adults.

The doctor smiled and looked at Zach slyly. "'Course, one look at their mother and you'll see why they're so cute."

Zach grunted. Now that was the part of meeting kids he didn't like—their mothers. Even the women who were married always seemed to have a scheme to get him married off to someone. You'd think there was something wrong with a man choosing to live in hotel rooms and wash his socks in bathroom sinks.

The doctor shook his head. "The poor woman. Such a pity—"

The doctor looked at Zach as though he expected some curiosity.

Zach had none.

The doctor ploughed ahead, anyway. "Jenny Collins is a widow. Not that she's old, mind you. No, sir. Moved up here a couple of months ago—surprised us

all. She'd been married to Jeb Collins's nephew.''
The doctor nodded at Zach as though Zach had
known this Jeb, whoever he was. ''Jeb had left the
place to his nephew, but we all thought the nephew
would have sense enough to sell it before he started
dying of that cancer of his. But he didn't. Don't know
what he was thinking. Surely he didn't expect his
widow to move up here with the two kids. What do
you think a city woman's gonna do with a place like
that anyway?''

Zach shrugged. He didn't like to get involved in
the problems of strangers.

The doctor had no such hesitation. ''Delores says
the woman's been getting magazines on farm man-
agement!'' He shook his head. ''She's a game one,
I'll give her that. But it's no place for her and the
kids—even old man Collins used to move into town
here for the winter months. The house doesn't even
have a decent road leading up to it. Ruts a mile deep,
and it drifts closed every time there's a blizzard.''

The doc took a breath before he continued. ''Delores always drives the mail right up to the house for
them. But with the next hard snow they won't get
mail for a week. The county snowplow doesn't go
that far out. Most farmers out that way have plows
on their tractors or something. But all the woman's
got is that car of hers—and with the two little ones—
Delores worries about their car not working.''

Delores, Zach had already learned, worried about
everything and everybody.

The doctor stopped suddenly and squinted at Zach. "What Jenny Collins needs is a husband."

Zach looked at the doctor in amazement and then pushed his hat farther down on his head. "Don't look at me. I'm just trying to get my horse fixed up. Besides, from the sounds of it, she needs a tractor worse than she needs a husband."

The doctor shrugged. "I doubt you'd stand a chance, anyway. I hear Max Daniel is planning to ask her out—he's a rancher north of here. 'Course Tom Fox might beat him to the punch. A good-looking woman like Jenny can have her pick of the bachelors around here."

Zach grunted. Ever since he started making money at rodeoing, he'd had women who wanted him to settle down. Made him nervous as a rope-tied calf every time a woman talked about it. Anyone with any sense could see that the life he'd led didn't prepare him for marriage.

Not that he didn't like women. He did. He just had sense enough to know his limitations. He didn't even have a year-round mailing address; he'd be a fool to think he would be any good at marriage.

"Yeah, well, it was only a thought," the doctor said as he pointed to the back of the truck. "Now, you remember what I said about the camera back there. Delores promised Jenny pictures of her little boy with Santa, and I'll never hear the end of it if you don't remember to take one."

"Pictures." Zach grimaced. "I'm not much good at pictures."

"What? You can't tell me that. Even I've seen your picture in the paper. You looked okay to me."

"Well, the news photos—and the ads—they're all right. But they're not, well, personal."

Zach didn't know how to explain his reluctance to have a picture of him in some family album along with pictures of babies and grandmas. He'd feel a fraud. A family photo album was one place he didn't belong.

"There's nothing to a Santa picture," the doctor said, pushing ahead anyway. "It's one of those cameras that prints out a picture while you wait. Jenny will even take the picture for you. And Delores said to leave it, in case Jenny wants to take other Christmas shots."

Zach nodded in defeat. What was Delores going for...mail carrier of the year?

"And don't forget about old Mrs. Goussley. She has a sweet tooth. Delores always gives her a few extra candy canes." The doctor winked "Say they're for her cats. She'll give them back if you say they're for her."

"Cats," Zach repeated bleakly. Forget mail carrier of the year, Delores must be going for sainthood.

"Mrs. Goussley likes her visit from Santa. She gets a kick out of the suit." The doc eyed Zach. "I know my sister got carried away this year with putting those flashing lights around Santa's belt, but you can keep them pressed off if you want. Plus the suit's warm—all that padding. Still it might not be enough. Gets cold out there. Could drop to zero before you get back.''

''I've got a sheepskin coat if it does.'' Zach had put his duffel bag and the coat in the postal truck. The sheepskin was imitation, but of good enough quality to be worth a pretty penny. It wasn't something he'd leave behind. Not that he didn't trust the doctor, but he'd worked enough rodeos to know never to leave his duffel with strangers.

''Oh, well then,'' the doctor muttered as he walked toward the truck. ''I'll just put this pie inside and let you get going. Remember, now, the brakes turn a little to the left if you happen to be going downhill.''

Zach nodded. He was definitely going downhill. Playing Santa to an old lady and her cats. Zach ''Lightning'' Lucas. He shook his head and pulled his Stetson down farther.

He sure hoped no one saw him.

Jenny Collins looked out the kitchen window again. Gray stormclouds almost covered the square butte west of her place. It was starting to snow, and the mail hadn't come yet. Delores had told her the doctor might be late with the mail, but he'd see the package got to them. It wasn't much, but it had the few presents she'd been able to get for the children, and she was anxious for them to arrive. Tomorrow was Christmas Eve day and, since it would be Sunday, there'd be no mail delivery then.

She had kept thinking she would get the car running, so Jenny had not sent her list in with Delores until a few days ago. The box should contain a water pistol for Andy, a paint kit for Lisa, and much-needed mittens and scarves for them both. Four-year-old Andy really wanted a cowboy outfit with a hat, and eight-year-old Lisa really wanted a princess tiara, but they were both too expensive and nowhere to be found in Deep Gulch anyway.

Maybe next year, Jenny consoled herself. She'd surely think of a way to make some money soon. She had to. She'd just spent everything except a few hundred dollars filling the propane tank so the furnace would keep going for the next few months. If nothing else, she wanted to be generous with heat when it came to their place.

Their place. She repeated the phrase to herself in satisfaction. This Christmas it would be enough that they had a home that was all their own, even if the roof leaked on the south side of the living room and the linoleum in the kitchen had more cracks than color left. Still, the place had three bedrooms and no mortgage. She was glad her husband had forgotten he had the deed to this place. It was the one thing she had left when the estate was settled.

She'd go looking for a job after Christmas. She'd have to go to Deep Gulch each day, anyway, once she enrolled Lisa in the school there.

Jenny had talked to the second-grade teacher, and they'd agreed Lisa could start in January. Surely by then Jenny would have the car running.

In the meantime, they were happy enough. Maybe more than happy. Jenny had always dreamed of living in a small town like Deep Gulch. Her dreams even included a mail carrier like Delores.

Jenny and her family had rented a house for eight years on that wretched street in El Monte, just east of Los Angeles, and the mail delivery people there changed routes so often she doubted any of them knew her face let alone her name. Here, Delores greeted Jenny like a friend and spoiled the kids with dinosaur candy and news of her own grandchildren.

Yes, Deep Gulch was home. Jenny just needed to find a way to make her piece of home support them.

''Mom, I see her coming!'' Andy's voice carried from the back bedroom. He was obviously looking out the window himself.

''Get down off those boxes, Andrew Joel.'' If he could see out the window, it meant he was standing on the boxes again. Jenny didn't intend to leave everything in boxes for long. She just hadn't been able to buy dressers or book shelves or cabinets—none of the furniture that stored things.

Jenny had left all their furniture in California. She'd had to. Their savings wouldn't stretch to paying off the funeral expenses and hiring a moving van, as well. Besides, she'd hoped there might be furniture in the house already.

That hope died when she took one look at the outside of the house and realized the inside probably wasn't much better. The property wasn't what she had expected. She doubted anything but thistle had grown on the place for the past ten years. The acreage was fenced, but half of the fence was down. The only trees were short scrub ones, and she'd already heard from someone at the store in Deep Gulch that the creek at the bottom of the coulee had been dry for the past five years.

· Still, Jenny knew this was their home. Even though it had already turned cold before they moved, the children liked to be outside. They had a freedom they had never known around Los Angeles.

If the children were happy, Jenny could live without furniture for a few months. She'd told the kids they'd pretend they were camping. So far, they hadn't complained.

"But she's coming!" Andrew said as he ran out of the bedroom door and down the small hallway. "She's coming to get my letter."

"Oh, dear. I forgot," Jenny remembered that Delores had promised Andy she'd take his letter special delivery to the North Pole so that Santa could read it before he began his trip tomorrow. Jenny had helped him write the letter so she had known for days what it said. She just hadn't realized he wanted the letter mailed until recently. "I'm afraid it won't be Delores getting the mail today. Her brother is taking the route for her."

"The guy who showed me that runny pig?"

"Runt. The pig was a runt. And, yes, that's the man."

"Can he find the North Pole?"

"I'm sure he can," Jenny said. Dr. Norris was a nice man. She was sure he'd play along with Andy's fantasy. Andy was at the age when he was starting to doubt Santa Claus, but he wasn't ready to give up hope yet.

Or maybe, Jenny thought, she was the one not willing for him to give up his fantasy. His young life had been so difficult. He'd never really had a father. At least not one who showed any interest in him.

Stephen had made it plain to Jenny even before they married that he wasn't a family man. Jenny had thought he would change—surely a man would care about his own children. But Stephen never had. Stephen had lived his life apart from the family as much as possible ever since her oldest, Lisa, was born.

No, it wouldn't hurt Andy to believe in Santa for another year.

Zach twisted the wheel to keep the postal truck on the road. The doctor hadn't exaggerated when he'd complained about the ruts to the Collins place. No wonder the woman's car was down for the count. There probably wasn't a nut or bolt in the vehicle that hadn't been shaken to within an inch of its life.

The road matched the house at its end. A bright patch of white paint around the door made the rest of the house look even more faded. He suspected this Collins woman didn't know that paint needed to be applied in warmer, dryer weather. Of course, he supposed it did get the message across that someone was living there. Without that paint and the yellow curtains in the kitchen window, the place would look deserted.

The land itself looked like no one had ever cared for it. Flat and gray, the land stretched out in all directions with nothing but half-melted lumps of old snow drifts and a few scrub trees on it. The gray patches were gathering a coating of white as the snowflakes started to fall. In the distance Zach saw a few buttes rising up from the ground, but they were so far away he didn't pay them any attention.

A woman opened the door as Zach pulled the postal truck to a stop. She was hugging an unbuttoned man's flannel shirt around her shoulders and was wearing a T-shirt and jeans. A young girl stood on one side of her and an even younger boy on the other.

Zach unlatched the side door and stepped out of the postal truck. The north wind was already turning bitter, so he walked along the south side of the truck until he reached the vehicle's back door. Cold, hard flakes of snow hit against his face.

Zach had given up and put the Santa beard and hat on before he even got to Mrs. Goussley's. It was the cookies that had done it. Every place he stopped someone shoved a plate of homemade cookies into his hands. He explained that he wasn't Delores—

shoot, he wasn't even the doctor—he wasn't entitled to any cookies. But no one listened. It was Christmas, they said, and he looked like a nice young man.

He hadn't been called a nice young man since he'd started riding rodeo.

He was getting soft, he thought glumly as he yanked the furry red cap farther down on his head and snapped the fake white beard into place. The cardboard box marked "Collins" and the pie were all the mail left to deliver.

Zach lifted the two things up. It would only take a minute to get the box up to the porch. Once there, he'd see about a quick Santa picture with the kids and head back to town. Maybe Thunder would be able to travel by then. If Zach was lucky, he'd be in the arms of that showgirl by Christmas after all.

Even from a distance Zach could see the woman was younger than he'd thought she would be. He'd guess her age at twenty-five or twenty-six. He shared the doctor's surprise that she'd taken on a farm in the middle of Montana. He would expect someone like her to move into one of the cities like Billings or maybe Missoula. Someplace that had a video store and a beauty shop.

Not that it was any of his worry. She could live on the moon for all he cared.

"Package," Zach said when he got close enough to the porch to thrust the package at the woman.

Short blond curls blew around her face, and up close he confirmed his opinion of her. Even in the cold, she would draw some attention in a crowd. The wind had turned her nose pink to match her cheeks.

Zach had a momentary wish he'd taken the Santa suit off before he'd made his last delivery. Lots of women had a weakness for cowboys. He'd never heard of a woman yet who thought a fat, polyester Santa was sexy.

Not that he was interested in what this woman or any woman in this part of Montana thought about him. What he'd told the doctor had been true—he was just delivering the mail and then passing through.

If Zach had been paying attention to what he was doing instead of admiring the woman in front of him, he would have seen her eyes sooner. Startled blue eyes looked straight at him.

"It's the mail," Zach clarified. No one else had greeted him with anything remotely like panic. Maybe she thought he was some kind of kook. "The suit's for the old ladies. Well, that and the pictures. Delores wanted you to have one with your kids."

"Where's the doctor?"

"Back in town looking after my horse."

"You've got a horse." The young boy looked around his mother's thigh and up at Zach. His eyes shone with wonder. "A real horse."

The two children stood on either side of the woman. The boy's jeans were neatly patched at the knees, and he obviously took his fair share of tumbles; the girl's clothes were well washed but showed no sign of stains or tears. Not even little ones. The boy's eyes had already welcomed Zach, but the girl's were more careful.

"Thunder's as real as a horse can be, even when he's sick," Zach said. "In his day, he was the best bucking bronc around."

"Santa has reindeer—not horses," the young girl pointedly corrected Zach as she crossed her arms. Zach pegged her age at seven. Maybe eight. "You need to get the story straight."

"It's no story," Zach protested. "I'm not—"

The woman's eyes widened in even more alarm and Zach stopped. He looked back down at the young boy.

"—in a hurry," Zach fumbled. Were there still kids left that believed in Santa Claus? Apparently so. "I'm not in a hurry at all."

The woman smiled in relief.

Now, *that* woman should smile more often, Zach thought. She was pretty without it, but when she smiled she made him think of one of those soap ads where they try to picture springtime. It might be twenty degrees below zero on this porch right now, but when he looked at her he could almost see the green meadow she should be walking through.

But, Zach reminded himself, he wasn't here to think of meadows. He was here to deliver the mail, snap a picture and give away the last of those blasted candy canes.

"I have something for you in my pocket." Zach had moved the last of the candy canes from the bag to his pocket several stops back. "Just let me set this box down inside the house and I'll get it out for you."

Zach didn't notice that the alarm on the woman's face turned to dismay.

"I can take the package," Jenny offered. She wasn't ready for company.

"No problem. I've got it," Zach said as he stepped up to the door the boy was opening.

"But I can—" Jenny started to repeat even as she watched the man walk into her kitchen. Great, she thought. Just what she needed—some man in a Santa suit seeing her house. Every man she had ever known expected a woman to keep a neat house. Stacks of boxes and fold-up furniture would hardly qualify as neat.

She hoped the beard would hide his disapproval. Although, she told herself with a tilt of her chin, it wasn't any of his business what kind of a housekeeper she was.

Chapter Two

"I haven't had a chance to get to town much yet," Jenny said defensively as she stepped through the kitchen doorway behind the man. She hadn't minded when Delores Norris had come inside and sat on one of the folding chairs. But a strange man was different. "I've been meaning to find some used furniture or something."

The man set the box and a foil-wrapped pie down on the kitchen counter and started patting his pockets.

The kitchen counter was covered with tiles so old the white had turned yellow, but Jenny had scrubbed the grout clean. The floor, too, was spotlessly clean even though the linoleum was cracked. No one could say the place was dirty, she reminded herself, even if they could say it lacked almost everything else to recommend it.

"I've asked about garage sales—then I'll be able to buy a few things," Jenny continued before realizing the man was not only not listening, but he hadn't even taken a good look around. He probably didn't realize that all that stood in the kitchen was a broom in one corner and the folding card table and chairs that sat square in the middle.

"I must have another candy cane here someplace." The Santa man turned and held up one candy cane. The plastic around the red-and-white cane was wrinkled and looked as if it had been slept on. "I'm sure I couldn't have given them all out already."

The man continued patting his pockets a little frantically. "I gave one for each of the cats—that was five—and a few extra when she said one of the cats was going to have kittens—and then she gave me that plate of cookies, and I had to give her some for that— but I should still have—"

Zach made another pass at checking the pocket on his right. The suit only had the two large pockets, and they had both been full of candy canes. He shouldn't have given so many to Mrs. Goussley and her cats. Not when two children were waiting at the end of the route. "Maybe one dropped out in the truck. I'll go see."

Zach smiled at the kids to show they could trust him. The boy smiled back, so excited he was almost spinning. The girl eyed Zach suspiciously. No smile there. She clearly had her doubts about him and the promised candy cane. Well, he didn't blame her. At least she wasn't whining about it.

Zach walked toward the door.

"I'll go with you," Jenny said, as she turned to the two children. "You two stay here."

"But, Mom, I gotta—"

"Stay here," the woman interrupted the young boy. "We'll be right back. I want to talk to Santa."

"But, Mom," the boy persisted. "I gotta—"

"Later. I need to talk to Santa *alone*." The young woman used her best mother voice. Gentle but firm.

Zach forgot all about the candy canes. Maybe Santa did have a little sex appeal if an attractive young woman was willing to take a walk in freezing temperatures just to talk to him privately. But he knew that a woman like her was trouble. He'd feel hog-tied after the second date. He'd have to tell her he was just passing through.

Zach took another look at the woman's face and hesitated. Maybe he was being too cautious about dating. Just because a second date was out of the question, that didn't mean a first date was impossible. Even a woman like that wouldn't have expectations on a first date, would she? A first date was a test with no commitment whatsoever. And that's all it would be. One date. He could put off starting down to Vegas until morning and still make it. Maybe he should ask her out for dinner tonight. He didn't see any restaurants in Deep Gulch, but people must go out somewhere.

"Where do people go around here for fun?" Zach asked as he opened the door for the woman.

It was only four o'clock in the afternoon, but the cold pinched at Zach's nose and he was grateful for the warmth of that beard on his face. The temperature had dipped a few degrees just in the time they had been inside. A full-fledged storm was coming.

"Fun?" The woman looked at him blankly. She crossed her arms against the cold and walked out the door, headed toward the postal truck.

Zach closed the door and hurried to follow. He could see the goose bumps on her neck in the strip between her collar and her hair. Pinpricks of snow still swirled around in the wind. "You need to wear something heavier than that flannel shirt when you're outside."

The woman walked faster. Her teeth chattered so he could hardly make out her words. "It'll do."

Zach opened the passenger door to the postal truck. The handle was icy to his touch. "Here. Sit inside."

Zach closed the passenger door and quickly walked around to the driver's side.

"You've heard of the North Pole?" the woman asked when Zach was inside and seated.

"That some kind of night club?" Zach was feeling more hopeful. Now they were talking fun. She didn't look like the kind of a woman to go to some pole-dancing night club, but you never could tell. Maybe he wouldn't even need to go to Vegas to find some

Christmas cheer. Pole dancing was as good as the showgirl stuff anyday.

"Huh?" the woman looked bewildered.

"The doc could watch the kids," Zach thought out loud. He felt a little bad about the kids, but the old doctor would treat them fine. He probably even had more of those candy canes. The kids could do without their mother for one night. Shoot, some kids would be glad to spend a night apart from their mother.

"The North Pole," the woman repeated as if she had doubts about his mental abilities. "You know— that place where Santa Claus makes his toys."

"Oh." So much for pole dancing.

Zach reached up and turned on the heat. The engine was still warm and gave off a soft wave of hot air. "I didn't know you meant *that* North Pole. Sure, I know it."

"Well, Andy is going to give you a letter to deliver to Santa Claus at the North Pole. Just go along with it, okay?"

"Sure," Zach shrugged. "I'll tell him I ride my horse, Thunder, right up there every night."

Jenny frowned. "Don't overdo it. He's four, but he's not gullible."

Zach refrained from pointing out that the boy still believed in Santa Claus. "Anything you say."

Zach smiled.

Jenny frowned.

Zach got a glimpse of himself in the rearview mirror and frowned, too. No wonder the woman was still cool to him. He looked like a lunatic. His beard was crooked and, instead of hair, it looked as if it were made of yarn that some cat had chewed. Zach pulled the beard down past his chin and let it settle around his neck. He pushed the Santa hat far enough back on his head so that she could see his hair. That should make her relax.

It didn't.

Jenny's frown turned to an expression of alarm. "You look just like that...that cowboy on the cereal box."

Zach relaxed. He was home free. She'd seen the Ranger boxes. "He's me—I mean, I'm him."

"But you can't be."

Jenny tried not to stare at the man's face. His cheekbones were high; his eyebrows black and fierce looking when he wasn't smiling. It was the middle of winter and his tan was only partially faded. The golden flecks in his brown eyes saved his face from being too severe. Nothing saved it from being the handsomest face she had ever seen.

Jenny had dreamed of that face ever since Andy had convinced her to buy the first box of that cereal a year ago. She must have bought three dozen boxes this last year alone. And that wasn't the worst of it. She'd been talking to the box.

Jenny was a private person and she didn't admit her unhappiness to anyone. But, one morning at a solitary breakfast, she'd poured out her troubles to the face on the back of the box and she'd been talking to it ever since. Only the face on the box knew of her disappointment with her marriage. To the rest of the world, her marriage was fine and her husband was the good-natured man he appeared to be to others. But the box knew the truth.

She'd told that box things she wouldn't have admitted to a priest, and now it sat before her. She felt betrayed. Pictures on cereal boxes were not supposed to spring to life in front of your eyes.

"—you just can't be him."

"Well, everybody's got to be somebody."

Jenny panicked. Not only was the face here, it was—unless she missed her guess—also teasing her. Maybe even flirting with her. It was awful—like the Pope asking you out on a date. "You'll have to go."

Okay, Zach thought to himself. Definitely not a pole dancer. Which was fine. He had his good time waiting in Vegas. "Just give me a minute to find another one of those candy canes and I'll be happy to head out. I need to get back before the storm hits anyway."

Jenny looked up. "I thought you said you'd take a picture with Andy."

"I did, but I thought you were, well, in a hurry for me to leave."

"No, I'm just, well, I don't want to take more of your time. But a picture only takes a second."

Jenny forced herself to look the man in the face. It wasn't his fault she'd started talking to his picture.

"Okay. Fine. Whatever you want."

Jenny forced herself to smile. "It's just that you're the only Santa around."

Zach grunted. "No problem."

"And I appreciate you bringing out everything for Delores. And the candy canes, too. That was very nice of you."

"Delores bought the canes. I'm just passing them out for her."

"Still…"

Zach noted that the woman's face had relaxed. The goose bumps had left. The air inside the truck wasn't white with trails of exhaled air. "Not a problem. I'll even tell that boy of yours I'll take his letter to Santa."

"I'm sorry I can't—I mean, I don't date anyway—not that you were asking me out." Jenny stopped in embarrassment.

"Oh, but I was asking you out. At least I was heading in that general direction."

Jenny couldn't help but notice he sounded a little too cheerful for someone who had just been turned down.

"Well, I appreciate that. I'm just sorry I can't accept."

"It's okay," Zach felt around the side of his seat and found not one but two candy canes. Hallelujah! He'd soon be out of here. "I suppose you tried the cereal and didn't like it—or you thought the manufacturer shouldn't say it is the cereal real cowboys eat when everybody knows cowboys don't eat anything but beans and trail dust.''

"No, actually, I like the cereal. And I think cowboys would like it if they had a chance to try it. It's great—real nutty.''

Zach nodded and didn't make the obvious comparison. "So you like the cereal. You just object to the box.''

Jenny nodded sheepishly. "I guess it is kind of odd.''

"No problem.'' Zach smiled to show it was okay. He'd been bucked by broncs. He'd learned how to take his lumps in life. If the woman was that set against him, he'd let it be. Better times were waiting for him. "I'll just take this other candy cane into the house and pick up the letter from—what's the kid's name again?''

"Andy.''

"So I'll pick up the letter from Andy, do our bit with the camera and be on my way back to the doctor's.''

"Thank you for understanding.''

Zach shrugged as he opened the driver's door on the postal truck. "Don't mention it.''

To show there were no hard feelings, Zach walked around and opened the passenger door, as well. "Some folks think the picture on the box is just some dress-up modeling job. But it isn't. The cereal company asked to put my picture on the box because I won the All-Pro Championship in bronc riding last fall.''

"Oh, I didn't think they used your picture because of your looks.'' Jenny gracefully stepped out of the truck and almost immediately folded her arms in front of her for warmth.

Zach admitted complete defeat. Most women found him attractive. He wasn't fool enough to go after one who didn't. Especially not when he was out in the middle of nowhere and the sky was turning a serious gray.

"Storm's coming,'' Zach offered as they walked toward the house. He suddenly understood why Delores worried so much over this little family. He felt some of that same worry tugging at him. There wasn't another house around for miles. "You got enough supplies stored up and everything? A winter storm in southern Montana can be a fierce thing.''

"I know that.''

Zach wondered how she could know that. He didn't ask, but she must have caught the drift of his disbelieving thoughts.

"I may not have lived through one of the storms here, but even in Los Angeles they have guidebooks that talk about Montana.''

Zach groaned inside. She'd learned about Montana storms from a guidebook.

The few snowflakes that were falling had a dry sting to them. Zach knew that meant the coming storm would be cold enough to freeze a person. Some folks thought the large wet flakes signaled the worst storms, but they didn't. The wet flakes generally meant more snow, but the dry ones foretold a swift and merciless drop in temperature. And with the wind that could be dangerous.

"The electrical will probably go out. Are you set for that?"

Jenny turned to look at him squarely and lifted her chin. She was standing on her porch and she could still feel the pinch of the cold in her nose. She could see the sky was going deep gray and she could hear the grumbling in the air. "We have a propane furnace. And I have some oil lamps if the lights go out."

Zach grunted.

The door on the house popped open when they stepped near it. Andy, the little boy, had been waiting for them to come back and must have heard their steps on the porch.

"Hi, there, Andy." Zach stepped inside behind Jenny. At least the little boy liked him.

Zach revised that opinion. The boy was looking at him like he'd sprouted a second head.

"Santa Claus?"

Zach grabbed for his chin. He'd forgotten the beard.

Jenny met his eyes in alarm. She took a quick breath. "Santa shaved."

Zach slipped the beard back over his chin. But it was too late. The kid was bewildered.

Then the confusion on Andy's face slowly cleared

as though he finally understood a big secret. Zach felt a momentary pang, but then decided it was just as well the kid learned the truth about Santa Claus.

Zach looked over at Jenny. She was signaling him desperately to do something.

Zach figured there wasn't much to be done.

"He'd find out someday anyway—now that he's a big boy." Zach threw the boy a bone. He knelt down until his eyes were level with the boy's. "Isn't that right? You're a big boy and big boys can handle the truth about Santa Claus, can't you?"

Andy nodded happily.

Zach threw Jenny a self-righteous look. He might not be a parent, but he did know some things about little boys. "You're a real smart big boy to figure out Santa's secret."

Zach noticed the girl who stood beside her mother. She rolled her eyes as if Zach was hopeless.

Andy nodded eagerly and leaned forward to whisper. "I know the secret. Santa's a cowboy—he's you—Lightnin' Lucas."

"Well, now, that's not exactly true." Zach stalled. Maybe he didn't understand a little boy's mind as much as he thought he did. "I am Lightning Lucas— that's true—but I'm just wearing a Santa suit. I'm a pretend Santa."

"I have cowboy pajamas," Andy nodded happily as he danced from one foot to the other. "That's pretend. Want to see?"

"Sure, I guess." Zach looked up at Jenny to get direction.

Jenny gave a reluctant nod. The pajamas had been Andy's present last Christmas and they were still his most prized possession. "Why don't you bring them out here and let Mr. Lucas see them when you give him your letter? I think he'll still take it for you."

Jenny lifted a questioning eyebrow at Zach.

Zach bristled. He was a man of his word. "Of course I'll still take the letter. I'll see the letter gets to the North Pole tonight. Before Santa leaves on his trip tomorrow. I'll take it personally."

"Can you fly?" Andy looked at him in awe. "Like the reindeer?"

Zach swallowed and shifted his weight onto his knee. "No, but I know the way to the North Pole and I can drive fast in my truck. Zoom. Zoom. Of course," he said, fumbling, "nobody should drive fast."

Zach hoped the kid forgot this conversation before he turned sixteen and got his driving permit.

"Will you take me with you?"

Zach looked over at the little boy looking at him with such shining trust. Like a shy deer, the boy had edged closer and closer to Zach as he knelt beside him until now the boy was practically leaning against Zach's shoulder. Zach had to swallow again. "Not this time."

"Why not? I'll be good."

Jenny looked down at the man and her boy and felt

sad. Andy yearned for a father even more than he yearned to be a cowboy. Maybe after Christmas she should accept a date from that rancher up north who kept asking her out. Even if Jenny didn't find him very exciting, he was stable.

Jenny had learned the hard way that exciting men weren't the best family men. She had a second chance to provide a father for her children, and this time she was going to choose carefully. Her children had never known the warmth of a real father. If she married again, it would be for them.

"Of course you'll be good," Zach said. "But you see, well, you have to stay and help your mother. There's a storm coming and she'll need a big boy like you to help her."

"Lisa's bigger. She can help."

Jenny looked at the helpless expression on Zach's face and almost laughed. Not many men were a match for a determined four-year-old.

"Of course she can." Zach searched the room for the girl and didn't see her. He wondered where she had gone. "It's just that—" Zach had an inspiration "—Santa's too busy to see people before he takes his trip. He only talks to the elves."

The boy looked up in sudden worry. "But my letter."

"Oh, I'm sure he has time for letters." Zach started to sweat. He decided he was better off facing a bucking bronc like Black Demon than a child like the one in front of him. He understood a thousand pounds of angry horse better than he did this little boy.

"I'm sure Santa reads all his mail," Jenny explained. Andy had labored for a full afternoon on his Santa letter, patiently copying the letters Jenny had printed for him.

Jenny hoped that Mr. Lightning understood how precious the letter was he'd offered to deliver. Andy hadn't thought of anything for days since he wrote that letter.

"Lisa can come, too." The little boy leaned closer to Zach and confided, "She told me there's no Santa at the North Pole." The boy's voice dropped to a whisper. "She has to do dishes for a month all by herself if I show her that Santa lives there. It's a bet."

Jenny saw her son's blond head leaning close to the man's dark one. The man's arm had gone around her son's shoulders and they were whispering about something she couldn't make out. She knew children liked their secrets, but she wasn't sure she wanted this cowboy to share them.

"Mr. Lucas needs to leave soon, Andy," Jenny reminded her son as she picked up the camera from the counter. Lisa had insisted she was too old for a Santa picture, so Jenny only had to worry about Andy. "Why don't you go get your letter for him, and I'll take your picture while you give it to him."

"It's here," Andy said as he moved away from Zach enough to pull a crumpled letter out of his pocket. He handed it up to Zach. "I've been saving it."

The camera flash went off as Jenny snapped a picture.

"I'll deliver it express mail." Zach blinked as he took the letter in his hand. The woman hadn't even given him time to force a smile. "You can trust the U.S. Postal Service." Zach saluted the boy even though, as far as he knew, the postal service had never had a salute of any kind. But it seemed to reassure the boy.

Zach stood up and looked at the woman. "If you want, you can try a second picture."

Jenny looked at him.

"I wasn't smiling." Zach almost swore. It wasn't his idea to have his picture in some family album, but if his picture was going to be there it seemed only right that he be smiling.

Jenny shrugged. "The beard covers most of your face anyway."

Zach nodded. If the woman didn't care if Santa was smiling, he shouldn't care. It did make him wonder what Christmas was coming to, however. If anyone should be smiling at Christmas, it was Santa and his helpers. "It's your picture."

"Did you get my letter in the picture?" the boy asked.

The woman nodded.

"I drew the stamp myself." The boy looked up at Zach. "Mom said it was all right."

Zach bent down and shook the boy's hand for further assurance. "It's just the right kind of stamp."

The kitchen had a window by the sink and one on the opposite wall. The sky was gray out of both windows, and Zach heard the rattle of the wind as it gathered force.

He watched as Jenny pulled the stub of a picture out of the camera.

"Here." Jenny held the camera out to him.

Zach shook his head. "The doc said you were to keep it over the holidays in case you want to take more pictures."

"Well, that's kind of you."

"Not me. It's Delores." Zach shuffled his feet. He wasn't used to getting so much credit for things he didn't even do.

"I better get out of here before the storm hits." Zach pulled his Santa hat back on his head. No one had flipped any light switches, and the light coming into the windows was thin. Fortunately, he could hear the hum of the furnace and a floor vent blew a steady stream of warm air into the room. At least the family had heat.

Zach looked over at the woman who held a still-developing picture in her hand. "You're sure you'll be all right now in this storm? If you need to call anyone on the telephone to come sit this storm out with you, I'd do it now. The lines might go down anytime now."

"Thanks. I'll do that." Jenny said. She smiled confidently as if she had someone to call.

Zach nodded. He figured that cereal box wasn't the only reason the woman wouldn't go out with him. She must have a boyfriend. Well, he shouldn't be surprised. The doctor had as much as told him she did. Some rancher—what was his name? Max something.

"Well, I'll leave, then," Zach said as he walked toward the door. "I'll close the door quick behind me so you keep your heat in."

Jenny watched the man walk to the door. Suddenly she didn't want him to leave. There was a blizzard coming and she didn't know what to expect. Even a cereal-box cowboy was better than no one when it came to facing a storm. But she couldn't ask him to stay. He was a stranger, for goodness sake. Just because she was used to telling her troubles to his face didn't mean he had any obligation to her.

"You've got holiday plans?" she squeaked out as he put his hand on the doorknob.

He turned around and looked at her. "Vegas."

"Oh. I see. Well, have fun."

Jenny could kick herself. Of course, the man had plans. It was Christmas, after all. Everyone had plans.

"Thanks." Zach hesitated. "I could change them if—"

"Of course you can't change them." Jenny stiffened her resolve. "I was just asking because I...I mean we…we have plans of our own and I was hoping you had plans, too.''

''I see. Thanks.'' Zach turned the knob this time. No sense staying where someone had plans that didn't include him.

Zach leaned into the wind as he walked to the postal truck. The sky was getting darker in the east. A spray of snowflakes hit his face, even with the beard pulled up. He noticed that he hadn't closed the back door to the postal truck completely. He walked over and snapped it shut. He didn't want a chill at his back while he raced this storm back to Deep Gulch.

Zach started the engine on the postal truck and released the brake. Time to get back. It was probably too late to beat the storm to the pass. Unless he missed his guess, he'd be sleeping in the horse trailer tonight while Thunder boarded at the doctor's barn. In a few hours no one would be doing much driving. Zach just hoped he made it back to the doctor's before the roads were snowed shut.

He could feel the hard boards of that trailer on his back already.

It was going to be some merry Christmas.

Chapter Three

Andy wanted a peanut butter sandwich.

"Just let me be sure the oil lamp is filled and I'll make you one," Jenny said as she watched the taillights of the postal truck pull away. The red lights were the only bright thing in the dark gray of the afternoon. A layer of snow had already fallen and she could see the tire tracks of the truck.

Jenny had made a mental list over a week ago of the things she needed to do to prepare for a winter storm. Making sure the lamp was full was the first one. The other was to be sure the curtains were drawn on all the windows so that there was a little extra insulation. Delores had insisted Jenny buy a case of beans and another of assorted soup when she moved here. The older woman had also urged her to always keep the propane tank that fed the furnace at least half-full.

"Heat and food is all you really need," the older woman had said. "If your pipes freeze you'll more than likely still have snow around that you can melt for water. Not that it's as pure as you might think. I'd get some water filters if I were you and run the melted water through them. Outside of that, keep healthy and you'll do fine."

Jenny didn't feel as if she was doing fine. She hadn't been able to get any filters for water. But the small stove in the kitchen fed off the propane tank out back so she could use that to boil snow water if necessary.

Just keep focused, she reminded herself. Like Delores had said, she'd do just fine.

Ten minutes passed before she realized Delores was wrong. Jenny wasn't fine. She'd made one big mistake. The number one rule of surviving a blizzard with your children was to actually have your children inside the house with you. Andy was here, but Lisa was gone.

Jenny had searched every room in the house twice before Andy confessed that Lisa had sneaked out the door in the laundry room and hid in the back of the postal truck. Jenny was accustomed to watching Andy. He was the one who got into trouble and scrapes. She never had to worry about Lisa.

"We got a bet going," Andy explained without a

trace of worry. "Lisa's gonna go see all about Santa and let me know."

Jenny's heart stopped. "You mean she went off alone!"

"The Lightning man's with her," Andy said calmly. "He'll take care of her until they get to Santa's workshop."

"But Mr. Lucas is going to Las Vegas!"

"Not until he takes my letter to the North Pole. He promised."

Jenny was speechless. Her daughter had run off with some cowboy on his way to Vegas, and she was only eight years old.

"He'll bring her right back," Jenny promised herself aloud. The man had to bring her back. "When he sees her in the truck, he'll bring her right back."

But what if he didn't see her? Lisa was obviously hidden or she'd be back already unless he was— Jenny stopped herself. No, she wouldn't even think that. She was sure he wasn't that kind of a person.

Jenny looked out the window. The tracks left by the postal truck had been filled in with new snow.

He's not going to see Lisa in time to bring her back, Jenny thought to herself in despair. Oh, she supposed he would leave her with Dr. Norris—when Jenny thought about it she had no worries that the man would actually want to take Lisa to Las Vegas with him—but still, Lisa would miss Christmas. Lisa had never been away from home at Christmas before.

Jenny looked around. She wished now that she had

swallowed her pride and asked someone to bring them a Christmas tree from town. She had told herself it would be okay for this Christmas to be plain. Her children would understand and share her gratefulness that they had a new home. They'd hang their stockings and read the Christmas story and that would be enough.

But she was wrong. Lisa wouldn't have come up with a ridiculous bet like this for Andy if they had both been busy decorating a tree or putting gumdrops on cookies. Her children needed Christmas and she had failed to give it to them.

Zach swore under his breath. The snow blew thicker every minute. And enough of it covered the road so that he couldn't make out the ruts. He was lucky to keep this tin can of a postal truck on the gravel road.

But the snow wasn't his big problem. His big problem sat on the passenger seat next to him.

"I knew you couldn't go to the North Pole," the girl said smugly as she bit into another oatmeal cookie. "There is no North Pole."

Zach gritted his teeth. "Didn't your mom teach you not to go off with strangers?"

He'd been halfway back to Deep Gulch when he'd heard the muffled sneeze from the back of the postal truck and had been so startled he'd almost driven off the road. In fact, he did pull to the side of the road so he could twist around and take a good look back there. The girl had been hiding under his sheep-skin coat.

"We're not in Los Angeles anymore." The girl took another bite of cookie. "There aren't any strangers here. Only farmers."

Zach had given her the plate of cookies he had gotten from Mrs. Goussley. So far she'd managed to polish off half of them.

"There are things to be careful about in Montana, too."

"I know." The girl brushed the crumbs off her jacket sleeve. "There's snakes in the coulee. And bees in the summer."

"And strangers. Weird people are everywhere. You can never be too careful with strangers."

The girl shrugged. "You got any milk?"

"Of course not, this is a postal truck not a lunch truck."

Zach strained to see through the snowstorm outside his windshield. He'd guess there was four inches of snow so far on the ground—maybe more. He hoped that was the final turn to the Collinses' place up ahead.

"Your mother's going to be worried. She won't know where you are."

"Andy will tell her. He can't keep a secret."

Zach hoped the girl's mother didn't jump to any wild ideas like that maybe he had asked the girl to come with him. He had given her the candy cane, but no mother would think that would be enough to entice a child to climb into his truck. Of course, he had said he was going to see Santa. A court of law might see that as enticement enough for any child.

Zach started to sweat. He'd best get this little one home soon. "Ah, good, that is the turn."

The snow was blowing so much he could only make out the outline of the house and the yellow glow of the windows.

Jenny thought she heard the sounds of a car and ran to the window. An hour had passed since Mr. Lucas had left, and the day had turned to evening. Jenny opened the door to see better. Stinging snow hit her face, but she only leaned out farther to try and see more clearly. If it weren't for those red and green lights on the postal truck, Jenny wouldn't have been sure it was Mr. Lucas coming back up her long driveway.

The truck stopped a few feet from the porch, and the lights went out. The driver's door opened and Jenny breathed easier. It was him.

"Lisa!" The wind blew the call away from Jenny and she wasn't sure her daughter would hear it, but the man did and he gave her a reassuring wave as he walked around to the passenger side of the truck.

Her daughter started to walk to the porch, but the wind made her stumble. The man picked her up and took her up the steps in long strides. Snow clung to her daughter's hair as the cowboy brought her across the porch and into the door that Jenny held open.

The temperature had dropped even more than Zach had figured when he was inside the truck. He knew that was why the girl clung to his neck. All that Santa suit polyester was warm and fuzzy. Still, he liked having her nestled there. It made him feel, well, a little fatherly, he thought defensively. Nothing wrong with that.

"Lisa! Are you all right, honey?" The woman opened her arms, and Zach reluctantly gave the girl to her.

"She's fine," Zach said curtly.

"I don't feel so good," the girl moaned.

"What'd you do to her?" Jenny shifted Lisa in her arms and glared at Zach.

"Me?" Zach looked around. Even the boy was looking at him suspiciously. "I swear. All I did was give her the candy and some cookies."

"You did find Santa's!" Andy gave a triumphant war whoop and jumped down off the chair where he was sitting. "No more dishes."

"The cookies came from Mrs. Goussley. Honest, you can call her up on the phone and ask her."

"That won't be necessary." Jenny set Lisa down on the floor and knelt at her eye level. "How many cookies did you eat?"

Lisa gave Zach a look of appeal.

"They were oatmeal cookies," Zach offered in her defense. He hadn't even counted how many were on that plate. "Oatmeal is good for you. Builds bones or something."

Jenny reached over and smoothed down her daughter's hair. It had been a long time since Lisa had been disobedient. Or done anything like eat too many cookies. It was good to see her daughter be a child again. "I guess a few extra cookies won't hurt anything."

A gust of wind rattled the house, and the overhead light flickered.

"I hope you have that lamp handy." Zach looked out the kitchen window. The sky was completely dark now, but he could see flakes of snow being whipped past the glass by the wind. "I should call the doctor, too, before everything goes down."

"The phone's over there." Jenny pointed to the wall opposite the sink.

"Did you get a chance to make your call earlier?" Zach stepped over to the phone. Whoever she had been planning to call earlier hadn't been much help to her. If she had called Zach with a storm like this on the way, he'd have been on her doorstep by now.

"I, ah, I thought I'd wait."

Zach pulled a slip of paper out of his pocket. The doctor had written his phone number on the same page he'd written the other instructions. Zach dialed.

"This is Zach Lucas." The phone only rang once before it was answered; the doctor must have been waiting for a call. "I'm at Jenny's—"

"Thank God someone's there! My sister's already called. There's a real blizzard coming through and she's worried—"

Another gust of wind hit the house and the phone went dead. Then the overhead light in the kitchen flickered again before it went out. Jenny's heart stopped. Her house was completely dark. There was no moon outside to provide a soft hint of light. There was nothing. Just the howl of the wind and the rattle of the windows. Followed by a whimper and the shuffle of little feet.

"Stay still, Andy, I'll come to you." Jenny said as she slid one foot out across the kitchen floor. Andy didn't like the dark. She had to get to him. He had nightmares.

"That's okay. I've got him," Zach said as he felt the boy's arms grab his thigh and hug tightly. Zach bent down to lift Andy up in his arms. "We're just fine, aren't we, partner? It's just a little darkness."

The boy burrowed into Zach's fuzzy suit. There was something about a Santa suit, Zach thought to himself. Even a crazy Santa suit like the one Delores had put together. It made the kids feel at home with him. He realized with surprise that he kind of liked it.

"I don't like the dark," Andy whispered softly.

"It's okay," Zach muttered as he shifted his arm so one of his hands would be free to feel the grooves along the belt of the Santa suit. If he remembered the doctor's words correctly, there was a switch here someplace that would turn on the flashing lights surrounding the belt. Zach had only seen the lights flash for a minute or two when the doctor first asked him to put on the suit.

Jenny kept taking small steps in the general direction of her son. What had made Andy slide over and grab on to the cowboy? She had been as close to Andy as the cowboy had been. "Mama's coming."

Zach's hand found the switch on the belt at the same time as he smelled the perfume. He stopped to take another breath. It was a simple perfume—peach, if he wasn't mistaken. But it made him want to keep the darkness around him for just a minute or two longer.

Jenny reached out to where she thought Andy was and touched the cowboy's arm instead. The softness of the Santa suit could not hide the solid steel of the man's muscle. Jenny knew she should move her hand when she discovered it was the cowboy she was touching and not her son, but she didn't. It was dark all around her and he was an anchor.

"Jenny?"

Jenny snatched her hand away from his arm. She was glad it was dark enough to hide the fierce blush she was sure was on her face. "I'm just worried about Andy."

"Of course," Zach shifted the boy's weight in his arms. "He's right here."

Jenny was close enough to sense the cowboy turning his body slightly so that her son was in the arm closest to her. Jenny reached out her hand again. This time she felt Andy's soft hair. She also felt the edge of Zach's shoulder.

It was ten degrees below zero outside and only about fifty degrees above zero inside the house, but Zach felt like he didn't need to see another fire again as long as he lived. Jenny's touch had been tentative, but it scorched him.

"Can you hold him while I get the lamp?" Jenny asked.

"You got oil in the lamp already?"

"It's right next to it." Jenny felt disoriented. The sink had to be in that direction. "Under the sink."

Zach groaned. "You better light me up, then, so you don't break your neck walking over there."

"What?"

"It's the belt," Zach interrupted. "It's got built-in Christmas lights. I had the switch a minute ago, but I had to let go when I moved Andy."

"But how do I?"

"Just feel along the belt until you come to a clicker kind of a thing. It attaches to the batteries."

"Your belt?"

Zach's mouth went dry at the breathless way she said it—as if he was asking her to do something a whole lot more intimate than turn on some lights. "It's about where Andy's feet are."

Jenny moved her hands away from Andy's hair and let them slide down Andy's back until the man shifted her son in his arms and suddenly her hands were sliding down the man's torso. Even the softness of the

Santa suit couldn't hide the lean muscles of his chest
and then his stomach underneath.

"I can't find it." Jenny stopped. It suddenly occurred to her she didn't want to go too low. But she
left her hand on his stomach. The whole world was
dark around her and she wanted an anchor. Besides,
she could hear his breathing.

Zach felt his breath catch. He shifted slightly to
balance Andy in his left arm. He put his right hand
over the one that Jenny had on his stomach. It wasn't
until he touched her that he felt her pulse. Her heart
was fluttering like a bird's.

"Scared?" Zach whispered.

"Me?" Jenny braced herself. It was only a man's
stomach for goodness sake. "No, I'm fine."

"Good. I'd begun to worry I scared you with what
I said about storms earlier. There's nothing to worry
about. We'll be fine."

Jenny had completely forgotten about the storm.
"Of course."

Zach reluctantly guided Jenny's hand to his belt
buckle. He realized he could have just flipped the
switch on his belt himself, but it was much more satisfying to feel Jenny's hand under his.

"I found it." Jenny felt the ridge of a button on
the side of the smooth plastic of the belt. She slid the
button to the right.

"That's it!"

A dozen tiny lights flickered. The kitchen was no

longer dark. Instead, long shadows filled the corners and a soft glow surrounded Santa.

"Mama." Lisa ran to Jenny and stood beside her.

Zach felt as if time had stopped. There was just enough light in the kitchen to see Jenny's eyes. Zach didn't even realize he was staring at her eyes until she blinked.

"I better go get the lamp." Jenny didn't move. She meant to move, but she didn't. In the light coming from Zach's belt, the man looked more like his cereal picture than he had since he'd pulled down his beard. It was his eyes, Jenny thought to herself. He was looking at her as if she'd just given him a championship trophy.

"I didn't know those lights would work so well." Zach tried to rein his mind back to the present. He would start counting to ten if he had to—he couldn't stand there staring at the woman. She'd think he was a lunatic.

"Oh." So that was it, Jenny thought. That's what pleased him so much. Men and their mechanical toys. "Yeah, they're something. Great lights."

Zach felt Andy squirm in his arms.

"I'm hungry," Andy said as he wiggled his way down Zach until he reached the floor.

"Let me get the lamp set up first." Jenny patted Andy on the head as she turned toward the counter. "Then I'll see what we can fix for dinner."

Jenny mentally catalogued the cans in her cupboard. She wished Delores had warned her to keep more than soup on hand for blizzards. She didn't have anything suitable for company. "I'm afraid it won't be fancy."

"I don't need fancy," Zach said.

One hour later they sat down to the table and there wasn't one hot thing on it. Even soup was impossible. "I never thought the pipes would be a problem."

The outside pipe on the propane stove had shaken loose in the wind. Zach had capped it off, but needed better light to fix it completely.

"This is just fine." Zach grinned. They were having cereal for dinner. His cereal. "I didn't know you ate this stuff."

"It's my favorite." Andy pushed his chair closer to Zach before he climbed up on it.

"I thought we should use some of the milk up since the refrigerator is off." Jenny set a plate of bread on the table and sat down. "I had a coupon for the cereal."

"So you're just trying the cereal out?"

"I wouldn't say that exactly." Jenny casually turned the cereal box so the man's face wasn't staring at her. "We eat lots of kinds of cereal."

"It's my favorite," Andy repeated as he picked up his spoon and waved it around. "Cowboys eat it."

"It's only your favorite because Mom bought a ton of it." Lisa unfolded the napkin by her plate.

"Mr. Lucas doesn't want to hear about what we eat." Especially not how much of his cereal we eat, Jenny thought frantically. "We should talk about—"

She tried to remember what single people talked about. "We should talk about— That's it..." Jenny turned to face the man. "How was your day today?"

Zach watched Andy take a spoonful of the cereal dry. He could hear him crunching away. "My horse got sick, but I ended up having a good time delivering the mail. Met some nice people. How was your day?"

"Oh, your horse. Did the doctor get a chance to say how he was before the phone line went dead?"

"I'm sure he's fine. It was just a low-grade fever." Zach noticed Jenny hadn't answered his question. Now what would a mother with small children do during the day? "I'll bet your day was spent getting ready for Christmas."

Jenny gasped and dropped her spoon on the table.

"What'd I say?" Even in the dark of the kitchen, Zach could tell he'd asked the wrong question.

"Nothing. It's just—" Jenny looked at her two children sitting one on each side of the stranger who should be a stranger but who wasn't because his eyes were looking straight at her just like he did from the cereal box. She couldn't keep it in any longer. She was used to making her confessions to that face. "I'm a terrible mother."

Zach saw the tear in her eye before she bent her head down, and he said the only thing he could. "That can't be true."

Jenny looked up at him. "I don't have a proper Christmas for my children, and that's why Lisa ran away with you."

"Lisa didn't run away with me. She didn't even run away, really. She had a bet she wanted to win."

"Yeah, Mama. I wouldn't run away. I just wanted to show Andy that there's no Santa at the North Pole."

"See what I mean?" Jenny wailed.

Zach half nodded. He didn't see at all, but he could tell the woman needed sympathy. "It's a shame they make all this fuss about a day—all it is is December twenty-fifth. Just the day after December twenty-fourth. No need to go on so."

Zach heard three gasps all at the same time. One good thing—he was pretty sure Jenny's tears had stopped.

"But Christmas is the birthday of Jesus," Lisa announced primly.

"All children need a Christmas," Jenny said at the same time.

"Don't you believe in Christmas?" Andy cut right to the important question. His eyes were wide in shock.

Zach squirmed and did the only manly thing he could. He lied. "Sure I believe in Christmas."

Jenny looked at him skeptically.

"Christmas just doesn't believe in me," Zach added softly.

"Well, surely you're going to celebrate Christmas," Jenny said. It was really none of her business, but everyone needed to celebrate something. And then she remembered that he was. "Of course, that's why you're going to Las Vegas."

Zach snorted. "I'm not going there to celebrate Christmas. I'm going there to forget there *is* such a miserable day."

"But I thought you had plans. That you were meeting a friend, or…" Jenny squinted at him. Surely nobody went to Las Vegas to be alone for the holidays. Come to think of it, it wasn't that easy to just go alone to Las Vegas at Christmas, especially without planning. "You won't get a hotel room, you know. Not over the holidays. All the hotels will be booked."

"Patti already has a room for me."

"I see." Jenny's voice tightened.

Jenny didn't know why she cared that the person he was driving hundreds of miles to see was a woman. And not just any woman. A woman with a name. She should be glad he was driving off to meet some woman. It would keep her focused. The last thing she or her family needed was a man like him around. They needed someone stable. Someone who would be a good husband and a father. "Well then, you don't have to worry about reservations."

Zach nodded.

Jenny knew she should let it go, but she didn't. "Maybe you'll see a show while you're there. I hear they have some wonderful Christmas shows."

"You're thinking of the family shows. The kind of show Patti and the girls do isn't what you'd call family fare."

"This Patti—she's a singer?"

Zach shook his head. "Naw, she's just one of the showgirls."

"With the feathers in her hair?" Jenny knew what those showgirls wore and didn't wear. "She must be very pretty."

"I suppose so."

Jenny stiffened. "Of course she's pretty. They all are."

Zach told himself Patti would have to be pretty. He'd only spent several hours with her last year. He knew she was a blonde. But outside of that... "I don't remember her eyes."

"Well, maybe you should try looking at her eyes instead of her—" Jenny broke off. Her children were at the table. Besides, it was none of her business who or what the cowboy admired. "Would you like some more cereal?"

"You know that showgirl stuff is mostly aerobics." Zach took the cereal box that Jenny offered.

"Aerobics?"

"Like cheerleading," Zach said firmly as he poured more cereal into his bowl. "Yeah, it's like cheerleading. Only with feathers and a bikini full of sequins."

"Mama was a cheerleader," Lisa offered proudly as she paused with her spoon halfway to her mouth. "Weren't you, Mama?"

"A long time ago."

"Really?"

"A very long time ago."

"We still have her pom-poms," Lisa said as she set down her spoon. "She didn't have any feathers or a bikini. She was a great cheerleader, though."

"I'm sure she was." Zach had a vision of Jenny bouncing around doing cheers. He wasn't sure it was at all the sort of vision he should have while he sat at the table with her children eating cereal. "She must have been wonderful—even without the feathers."

Jenny could feel the blush on her cheeks. She needed to change the subject. "The snow should be gone by tomorrow. It's too early to have a blizzard that sticks. You should still be able to make it out of here and catch your show."

Zach looked at her as if she was crazy. "What makes you think that?"

"The guidebook says—"

Zach snorted. "You have that guidebook here? Let me see it. I can practically guarantee you that this blizzard will last forty-eight hours."

"But that's impossible." Jenny looked stunned. "Montana doesn't have long blizzards before Christmas."

"Tell that to the sky," Zach said.

Jenny would tell it to the sky if she thought there was any hope the sky would listen. "So you'll be here for Christmas."

"Looks like it."

"I'm afraid it won't be nearly as exciting as Las Vegas," Jenny said. Surely he would be able to leave tomorrow. The postal truck was a four-wheel-drive. It could go places her car couldn't go even when it was running. The house suddenly felt much too small, and the Christmas she'd planned much too humble to share with this man. "We don't even have a tree."

Zach felt the collar of his shirt get smaller and he swallowed. "I'm not worried about a tree. They aren't anything but a fire hazard anyway."

"You don't like Christmas trees?" Lisa asked him in a voice that suggested he hated babies.

"Well, I...I don't have anything against them, I guess." Zach tried to make amends. "Especially if they don't have lights on them."

"No lights!" Lisa scoffed at him. "If there's no lights, it's not even a Christmas tree. Everyone knows that."

Jenny knew she should have tried harder to get a tree. Christmas was important to children. Well, it wasn't too late. "I'm going to go out tomorrow and get us a Christmas tree."

"Really?" Lisa turned to her mother breathlessly. "You are?"

"Of course," Jenny said. "This is Montana. There's lots of trees around. It might not be a pine tree like the ones we used to have in Los Angeles, but I can find something to decorate."

"It'll be ten below zero tomorrow." Zach thought he should mention the fact. "You'll freeze to death."

"Tomorrow will be a fine day." Jenny lifted her

chin. "Montana blizzards this time of year never last."

Zach groaned. Even if the sun did shine tomorrow, he couldn't leave this family in this kind of weather. They'd never make it through Christmas without help the way they were carrying on. Jenny would freeze out there trying to chop down some fool sage bush. "And don't try baking any Christmas cookies until that propane line is fixed."

"Cookies," Andy sighed blissfully as he looked at Zach. "Are you going to make us some Christmas cookies?"

"Me?" Zach didn't like the trusting look in the boy's eyes. "I don't cook."

"I'll help you," Andy said, his trust not wavering. "I know how to stir. We can make cookies, can't we, Mom?"

Jenny looked at her son. She'd never seen him this anxious to spend time with a man before. It must be because Zach was a cowboy. How could she explain to her son that this man was not the kind of man to put on an apron and bake cookies with a little boy. "Mr. Lucas might be busy."

Fortunately, Andy didn't ask what the man would be busy doing. "Busy" was the excuse his father had always used when Andy asked to do anything with him.

Zach watched the joy flow out of Andy's eyes, and he found he didn't like it. "I guess I could learn to make cookies. How hard can it be?"

"Really?" Andy's eyes shone again.

"What?" Jenny's eyes stared at Zach like he'd offered to fly to the moon. "Are you sure?"

Zach nodded. He wasn't going soft, he told himself. He was snowed in with this family. Stranded, really. He was just making the best of a bad situation. Anyone would do the same. It was that time of year, after all.

He sure hoped he wasn't going soft.

Chapter Four

Jenny had no choice but to follow the cereal cowboy and her son deeper into the house. They'd all cleared their bowls off the card table, and there was nothing to keep them in the kitchen.

"We've only been here a little over a month." Jenny carried a flashlight even though Zach and his lit belt showed everyone the way.

The living room was almost empty. She had a cork bulletin board hanging on one wall that was covered with snapshots of the kids, but it was the only thing hanging on the walls.

A few boxes stood along the other wall. The flaps of the boxes were pulled up and showed a jumble of children's books. They didn't have television so the children each picked a favorite story each night and they sat together while Jenny read to them. Lisa loved fairy tales. Andy liked animal books.

"We're camping," Andy confided in a loud whisper as he led Zach through the living room. "That's why we don't need no furniture."

Jenny winced. The one piece of furniture that had been there to welcome them was a rust-colored sofa that sagged and had a grease spot on the right cushion. Jenny had covered it with a light-blue afghan she had knit when she was pregnant with Andy. It was a baby's afghan, but she'd made it large and it almost covered the sofa. "I plan to get some used furniture just as soon as I can get to Billings."

"Yeah, I hear your car isn't working," Zach said as he followed Andy's lead and sat down on the sofa. "Doc Norris said it was the radiator."

No sooner had Zach settled on the sofa than Andy burrowed into the cushion next to Zach's elbow and whispered, "The doctor—he's got pigs."

"Is that right?" Zach looked down at the boy. The living room was full of crazy red and green shadows from the Christmas lights on the Santa belt, but no matter what shade of light surrounded the boy's face it just seemed to keep shining. Zach had a pang of wistfulness knowing he'd never been that trusting. Certainly not at four years old. Maybe not even at four months. Not with the kind of parents he'd had. He'd had to learn to take care of himself early. By the time he was Andy's age, he was taking care of his alcoholic parents as well as himself.

"I've got pigs, too," Andy said as he jumped off the sofa and headed toward the books. "They huffed and puffed."

Zach felt as if he'd fallen down a rabbit hole.

"It was the wolf that huffed and puffed," Jenny clarified. She had to admit that the cowboy was taking her sparse furnishings better than she would have expected. He didn't look around with anything like pity in his brown eyes.

Andy found the book he was looking for and waved it at Zach. "Read me the story."

"Mr. Lightning might not have time." Jenny wished Andy wasn't so intent on relating to the cowboy. She supposed Andy would be that way with any man these days. But a drifter like Zach would have no patience with a little boy, and she couldn't bear to see Andy hurt. "He's resting."

Andy put his book down easily and looked at Zach with round eyes. "Is he sick?"

Zach heard Jenny's quick intake of breath at the same time as he saw the worry flare in Lisa's eyes as she stood next to her mother. Then he remembered what the doctor had said about Jenny's husband dying of cancer. "Don't worry. I'm not the kind of guy who gets sick. I'm healthy as a horse."

"Your horse is sick," Lisa reminded him as she walked over to the books and stood next to Andy.

"That's just Thunder's disposition," Zach said. He couldn't help but notice how the girl came close to him, but not too close. "He just likes to complain about his aches and pains. He's not a sunshine guy like me.''

Zach saw the quick smile that crossed Lisa's face before she rolled her eyes.

''Let me see that book,'' Zach held his hand out for the book Andy had picked up again. He patted the sofa on the side opposite where Andy sat. ''No reason we can't all read it together. I've always wondered about wolves. Thought I might get one for a pet one of these days.''

''Wolves aren't pets,'' Lisa informed him. She sat down next to Zach, but her back was straight and she perched cautiously on the edge of the sofa. ''They're dangerous animals.''

Zach had no idea how it happened, but the wolf led to some ballerina Lisa was anxious for him to read about.

''She has a tiara,'' Lisa told him solemnly as she pointed to the shiny circle on the girl's head in the book. By this time, Lisa had snuggled close to his other elbow.

''She looks like a real princess,'' Zach agreed. Zach decided he liked being enclosed by the kids. Now if only Jenny would join them on the sofa.

Jenny sat on a folding chair and looked at the cowboy and her children. She could not remember a scene like this one in her whole life. Even if her late husband, Stephen, unbent enough to relate to one of the kids, he never included them both at the same time. He certainly never read to them.

It was past bedtime for Andy, but Jenny let the time pass. If it wasn't that she thought she might destroy the moment by capturing it, she would take a picture of the three of them. Her children would remember this cowboy reading to them for a long time.

"I asked Santa for a tiara," Lisa sighed as Zach finished reading the last page of the book. "But it's too expensive."

"Santa doesn't need money," Andy said cheerfully as he wiggled even closer to Zach. "He's got elves. They'll make you up one of those things."

"Elves can't make tiaras," Lisa said as she straightened her back and took the book out of Zach's hands. "They don't have any jewels. You need jewels for a tiara."

"Oh." Andy thought about this. "But they have cowboy stuff. Cowboy stuff doesn't take jewels. You could ask for some of that, like me."

Lisa stood up to take the book back to the box. "I hope you didn't write that in your letter. If I can't have a tiara, I at least want something that's pretty. I don't want anything cowboy."

Jenny knew what was coming and tried to head the question off before it was formed. "Time for bed, Andy." Jenny stood up and added another distraction. "You can wear your cowboy pajamas." Jenny kept her voice cheerful and calm, but she could see the frown forming on Andy's face.

"When are you going to take my letter to Santa, Mr. Lightning?" Andy asked in a soft voice. "Lisa said you had to bring her back. You never got to the North Pole.''

Zach reached out automatically and patted the pocket that held the letter. Oh, oh. He'd forgotten it was still there. He looked to Jenny for help.

''Mr. Lightning did his best,'' Jenny said softly as she walked over to her son. ''But there's a blizzard outside. The roads are all full of snow. He had to turn back before he got to the North Pole.''

Andy looked up at Zach in alarm. ''But you're still going to take my letter, aren't you? It's almost time for Santa to come. He has to get my letter or he won't know what to bring me.''

Zach knew he was a sucker. There was no longer any doubt. ''I'm just waiting for everyone to go to bed. Then I'll crank up the old truck and make a quick trip.''

Andy looked up at Zach in relief. ''It won't take long. You can go fast. Zoom, zoom. You said so.''

''That I did.''

Lisa rolled her eyes and Jenny opened her mouth to protest, but neither of them said anything.

''The quicker you get to bed, the sooner I can get going to the North Pole,'' Zach said.

Jenny had never seen her son so anxious to get to bed. Andy ran into his room and changed into his pajamas in the thin streaks of light that shone into his room from the living room. Even Lisa seemed content to go to her bedroom.

Jenny had managed to get a single mattress for

each of the bedrooms, but she hadn't prepared for company. "I'm sorry, all I have to offer you is the sofa."

Zach smiled. "The sofa's fine."

"It's really not too bad," Jenny apologized as she went over to a box and pulled out several wool blankets. "And I have some blankets, of course, that you can use. I don't have a spare pillow, but we can roll a blanket up and—"

- "It's fine," Zach repeated.

Jenny had been worrying. The Santa letter had become more complicated than she'd ever imagined. "Andy can be persistent."

"That's a good thing."

Jenny kept her voice low as she put the rolled-up blanket at one end of the sofa. "We'll just tell him in the morning that you went to Santa's while he was asleep."

"You think he'll believe that?" Zach whispered in amazement. "If I know him, he's going to lie awake in there until he hears me leave." Zach shook his head in pride. "He might only be four, but he's awfully sharp."

"But what else can we do?"

Zach no longer bothered to lower his voice. "In just a few minutes, I'm going to go out to my truck and start driving it away."

"Oh." Jenny knew she shouldn't have expected him to stay. "I see."

Jenny swallowed before it occurred to her that even

if the man wasn't the kind who stayed around, he didn't look like the kind who was crazy enough to head back to the main road in this weather.

"There's a blizzard out there," she whispered just in case he had forgotten. "You won't get halfway to Deep Gulch without getting stuck."

"Ah." Zach smiled and winked at her. "But I don't need to get to Deep Gulch. I only need to get to the North Pole."

They both heard the sigh of deep contentment that came from Andy's room before they heard the boy's voice. "It won't take long."

"No, it won't, partner," Zach agreed as he stood up. "It won't take long at all."

"Mom can go with you," Andy offered from the bedroom. "Just in case you have trouble on the way back. She knows the way back here real good."

Now that's an idea, Zach thought to himself, before he realized how unlikely that would be with the kids in bed. "Your mom probably needs to stay with you."

Zach glanced sideways at Jenny just in case she was the kind of mother who was willing to leave her kids alone on a dark night so she could go for a freezing-cold drive with a bachelor.

Zach had known women who would have left their kids in strip joints if it meant they could spend time with a cowboy. Not that he was passing judgment on those women. He knew plenty of men who were just as irresponsible. Who was he fooling? He *was* one of those men who were just as irresponsible.

"It sure would keep me warmer if I had some company," Zach said softly as he followed Jenny out into the kitchen. If Jenny was the kind of mother willing to leave her kids, she'd be the kind of woman to give him a friendly kiss or two out there under the night sky. He had a sudden, powerful urge to know if her wide blue eyes changed colors and danced with stars when she was kissed. "I wonder how cold it is out there, anyway."

"Give me a minute and I'll let you know. I've gotten pretty accurate at guessing temperature." Jenny turned back to look at Zach.

Zach stepped closer. He wondered if Jenny could tell how much the kitchen had heated up since she'd turned to face him. He knew his temperature had risen by ten degrees. Her face was dusted with pink. And it was more than the red in the lights at his belt. The kitchen was still in shadows but her face looked petal soft. He could almost taste those kisses. He figured her for a sweet kisser. He couldn't wait to find out just how sweet.

It took a second or two for Zach to get past his thoughts of kissing and realize Jenny was willing to leave the kids and go off with him for a long ride into the night. It took another second for his disappointment to settle. He'd have wagered his saddle that she was a better parent than that. Not that his disappointment would stop him from showing the lady a good time, he told himself. "It doesn't matter how cold it is out there, I'll keep you warm."

Now that Zach realized Jenny wasn't a saint, he figured the same old lines would work with her that he'd used in the rodeo for years. He was back in the game.

Jenny rolled her eyes, but didn't even respond to him. She just turned and walked toward the far kitchen wall. "I hope you don't mind if I drive the postal truck. The kids will be fine with you here."

"What?" Zach couldn't believe it. He was still stuck in his fantasy of her hot lips in the cold night. What had she said? He followed her through the kitchen. "You're going without me? Without me? Out there—into that blizzard?"

Was the woman crazy?

"Do you know how cold it is out there?" he asked, just to be sure. "It isn't anyplace for a woman alone—not on a night like tonight. This windchill is nothing to mess around with—especially for a woman alone."

Zach knew he had said the wrong thing even as he saw Jenny bristle. She turned to face him.

"Actually—" Jenny's voice was chilly enough to match the outdoors "—a woman alone is just fine—inside or outside. Especially if she's read her guidebooks. The fact is women are better suited for the cold than men."

Zach lifted his eyebrow.

Jenny put her chin up in the air slightly. "It's true.

It's because of body fat. Women have more body fat.''

"But only in—'' Zach stopped. He wasn't sure Jenny would like him to tell her where her body fat was stored. Especially since it was in places that were causing him some discomfort now that the idea of kissing her had taken hold of him with a vengeance. Maybe he was the one who was crazy here.

Jenny turned and reached up to the coat hooks that were next to the door. "Well, we both can't go." Jenny lifted off a drab blanket that was hanging on the hook. She'd grown accustomed to being both mother and father to her children years ago. "I wouldn't expect a stranger to do this for my children. It's my responsibility. Besides, I should have gotten the letter to Santa some other way before you came. It's not your problem.''

The kitchen windows all looked out at the black night. Zach took a breath.

"It might not be my problem, but it is my truck." Zach put his hands on his hips. Let her argue with that. "I'll drive the thing.''

"You hate that truck. You said so earlier." Jenny wrapped the blanket around her shoulders like a shawl. "Besides, we both know it's not your truck. It belongs to the post office.''

"That truck is entrusted to my care," Zach said stubbornly. He'd moved his hands away from his hips. The extra Santa padding under that suit he still wore made him feel ridiculous. "The doctor didn't say anything about me lending it out to folks to go driving around in it like it's some kind of do-it-yourself taxicab.''

"I'm a good driver," Jenny held out her hand for the keys. "You can wait in the kitchen until I get back so the kids think you're gone, too. Just keep an eye on that furnace."

"Well, if they think I'm gone, maybe I should be."

"Somebody needs to be here in case something goes wrong." Jenny flashed Zach a smile. "Don't worry—the kids won't be a problem. They don't come out of their beds once they get settled. That's one good thing about it being cold. They don't want to leave their bed once they get the sheets warm."

Zach's frown turned to a scowl. Speaking of sheets, something was wrong with that blanket Jenny was holding like a shawl. "Is that what you use for a coat?"

Jenny lifted her chin as she wrapped the blanket more closely around her shoulders. "We used to live in Los Angeles. It wasn't cold enough there to need heavy coats."

"Well, this isn't Los Angeles." Zach looked at the other two hooks. They both held new snow coats, one in pink for Lisa and one in red for Andy. "You should have bought a coat for yourself when you bought the ones for the kids."

Jenny shrugged. "The kids needed the coats more than I did. I can get by until spring."

Zach didn't say anything. Boy, was he wrong to

think she was an irresponsible parent. She was halfway to sainthood. Which made him proud in a funny
sort of a way. Until he figured it out. If she was that
kind of woman, his odds of getting a free kiss in this
house were about the same as they would be at a PTA
meeting filled with Republican grandmothers.

He'd learned long ago that kissing good women
was complicated. They tended to take their kissing
seriously. A kiss or two and they started thinking
about china patterns and meeting your family. Zach
didn't even know where his parents were anymore.
Even if he did know, he sure wasn't going to take
any woman to meet them.

Jenny lifted the blanket up to wrap it around her
head as well as her shoulders.

"Andy asked me to deliver his letter." Zach pulled
up the collar on his Santa suit. His hopes of a kiss
might be gone, but he still would do this his way.
"I'm responsible for the U.S. mail. I'm the one who's
going."

Jenny looked at the man. The kitchen was in shadows, but she had no problem seeing the face before
her. Faint red lines marked his cheek where the Santa
beard had rubbed. A strong chin was brushed lightly
with late-day whiskers. Brown eyes met hers with de-
termination. She'd seen that same steady look in his
eyes in rodeo pictures of him on those cereal boxes.
He made one fierce-looking Santa.

"But it's cold out there."

"Then make me something hot to drink when I get

back.'' Zach reached for the knob on the door. He wasn't going to argue on this one. He wouldn't be able to think straight if he let her take off in a night blizzard while he stayed in the kitchen. What kind of man would he be if he did that?

"I don't know what to say," Jenny tried again. The blanket around her shoulders was stiff, but she held it firm. "You shouldn't have to do this. You don't even like Christmas.''

"Yes, I do." Zach gritted his teeth. What was it about this family? "I just don't see the need to go overboard and fuss about everything.''

"You mean fuss about things like delivering a child's Santa letter?" Jenny asked softly.

"Well, no. The letter, now that's important. U.S. Postal Service business. I'm just doing my job.''

Jenny smiled. "You're losing money. There's not even an official stamp on the envelope.''

"It's official enough for me." He paused and added, "Besides, I gave my word. He's counting on me.''

Jenny was speechless, and Zach took that as sign enough to open the door and leave.

The cold outside air lingered briefly inside while Jenny stood at the door's window and watched the red and green lights bump their way down her driveway. So that's what this man did when he gave his word. He actually carried through with his promise.

All Jenny saw of the postal truck was lights. She could, of course, hear the truck. She suspected Zach revved the motor a little extra just so it was very obvious that he was driving away.

Jenny was amazed. This cowboy was actually honoring his word. Her late husband had only considered promises made to adults to be binding. And then only if the adults were other men. Jenny was beginning to wonder if she hadn't misjudged the cereal-box cowboy. Not that it would make much difference. A man with that much sexual magnetism was not the kind of man she wanted in her life the second time around.

If and when she married again, she would marry for the sake of her children. And she wouldn't take any chances. She'd marry a solid citizen. Maybe a banker. Or a schoolteacher. A teacher would be nice. But a cowboy? Not a chance.

Jenny pulled the blanket closer around her shoulders as though she could press the heat into her skin. She wished the cowboy had let her make the drive. She felt beholden enough to him already and didn't relish adding a favor like this to the list. She had her pride. She just had no way to repay him.

Unless—Jenny still had a few dollars in the bank. She could write him a check. Yes, a check, she thought to herself in satisfaction. A check should even the score nicely.

Outside in the cold, Zach stopped the postal truck. He'd driven a quarter of a mile away from the house when he stopped and turned out the lights, just in case Andy had watched him leave the house. He'd leave the lights off for a few minutes so that it would look like the truck was far, far away on its way to the North Pole. He knew Jenny had said that the kids both stayed tucked into bed once they were down, but he also knew that Christmas changed the rules for kids everywhere.

Without the heater on, the temperature inside the postal truck dipped quickly. If Jenny was sitting next to him, Zach knew he'd ask her what the temperature was just to challenge her skill. He smiled. She was some amazing lady. He wondered if she really could tell temperatures like that.

The black night, even with the cold outside, was peaceful. Zach clicked on the lights on his belt so he could read his watch. He'd had the lights off for five minutes. He wondered how long a kid would figure it would take to go to the North Pole.

Speaking of the North Pole, Zach pulled out the letter Andy had written. He wasn't curious about what the requests were. The kids had already told him what they wanted. But he was beginning to worry.

The box he'd brought out to this family hadn't been heavy enough to satisfy any child's Santa wish. Besides, he knew what was in it. The camera, a frozen ham that Jenny had already put in the unheated laundry room, the pie from Delores Norris, and two small brown bags from the one store in Deep Gulch.

Those brown bags looked awfully puny.

Zach sat in silence. He knew firsthand how it felt to be disappointed at Christmas. He'd never believed

in Santa Claus, but when he was ten years old someone had sent his parents a Christmas card with a family picture on the front of it. Everyone in the picture
was standing beside a Christmas tree and looking
happy. That was Zach's first glimpse of what the day
was like for other families, and that Christmas Zach
had decided Christmas should be that way for his
family.

Zach had begged a scrawny leftover tree from a
nearby lot on Christmas Eve and set it up in the living
room. He'd thought a tree would make the difference.
He'd believed the tree would turn his family into a
Christmas family like the one on that card. But his
parents had only used the tree as an excuse to drink
more than usual, quarreling over who should propose
the next toast to it.

No one in his family smiled that Christmas and
Zach threw the tree away the next day. That was the
last time he had had any hopes at Christmas. But he'd
never spent Christmas with children like Andy and
Lisa. They were good kids. They deserved a good
Christmas.

Zach did not know exactly when in the darkness
the idea came to him, but it somehow did. He, Zach
"Lightning" Lucas, knew what the children wanted.
They knew that he wasn't the real Santa but they had
still both trusted him with their Christmas wishes.

Maybe it was time Zach lived up to the red suit he
wore. In this snow-covered corner of Montana he was

Santa. He would see that their hoped-for presents were delivered.

At first Zach thought about driving into Deep Gulch tomorrow, but then he realized he had the same limitations that had faced Jenny. The one store in Deep Gulch, a multipurpose little store with everything from bread to automotive oil, would not have either Lisa's tiara or Andy's cowboy outfit.

Of course, the cowboy outfit—Zach looked into the back of the postal truck. His duffel bag was still there along with his sheepskin coat. He hadn't packed much for his trip to Vegas, but he did have the latest championship buckle in there that he had just won last month.

He knew how to work with leather and he had a broken bridle in his duffel that he'd been meaning to fix. He might be able to fashion a belt for the boy. And he could put a thick lining in his Stetson hat to fit the kid. He didn't have a toy gun, but he could make a small rope with some of that postal twine in the truck.

Lisa's tiara would be more difficult. Especially because, as she'd reminded Andy, a tiara needed to have jewels.

Zach grinned to himself. Now that he thought of it, he did have jewels. Zach reached into the back and pulled the duffel toward him. He unzipped the bag and felt around in the contents until his hand found what he was seeking. He'd brought a Christmas present for Patti.

He twirled the lacy leg garter on his finger and grinned.

The showgirl would never miss the fancy garter he'd bought her. But Lisa would love the rhinestones that circled it. There were pink rhinestones and clear rhinestones and small pieces of ruby. And, if Jenny had a metal clothes hanger that he could bend, he'd be in business.

By the time Zach turned the engine back on in the postal truck, he'd decided that this Christmas might be tolerable after all. Imagine Zach "Lightning" Lucas filling in for Santa Claus.

Zach ho-ho-ho'ed to himself just to see if he had the knack.

He didn't.

But that didn't matter. Zach would pretend to have the Christmas spirit even if it killed him. He'd do it for the sake of the kids.

He only hoped Jenny would cooperate.

Chapter Five

Jenny looked out the window again. It had been totally black outside the last time she'd peeked, but now she could see the lights of the postal truck coming closer to the house.

Jenny was beginning to have second thoughts. She'd looked at her bank book, and the crude budget she'd worked up to see them through the winter, before deciding to write the check for seven dollars. It wasn't much, but it was all she dared give away until she knew how much it would cost to fix the radiator on her car.

The truck engine came to a stop near the house, and Jenny smoothed back her hair. She'd put some water into her fondue pan and lit the candle underneath. She didn't know how long it would take the water to heat, but she intended to have a hot drink for Zach when he came inside. That and the check would make her feel less indebted to him.

Zach sat in the postal truck. While he was driving back up the path that led to Jenny's house he'd noticed the ball of mistletoe Delores Norris had hung on the antenna of the truck. It would freeze solid if he left it outside over night. He might as well haul it in with his gear.

Zach opened the door and stepped outside into the snow.

The night was kinder to Jenny's house than the light of day had been. In the dark, the flickering light through the kitchen window gave the house a warm look, as if someone was waiting up for the last one of the family to come home.

Maybe, Zach thought wryly, that's why he preferred busy hotels. With all the neon flash of a hotel at night, everyone knew there was nothing personal about the fact that someone was waiting up inside. It was strictly business. Zach liked it that way.

If no one was waiting up, there would never be anyone to be disappointed when they discovered that Zach knew absolutely nothing about the things other people took for granted. The Christmas tree failure had only been one lesson he'd learned as a child. It was that same year he'd discovered other families ate their meals together at a table. He'd asked his mother if they could do the same. One meal together had cured them all of the idea.

No, Zach knew he wasn't meant for family life.

Not that he usually thought about such things, Zach told himself with a shake of his head. He'd made peace with his limitations many years ago. He wouldn't wish the life he'd had growing up on anyone, but that was what he knew. Zach figured he was destined to follow in his parents' footsteps, and it wasn't a path he wanted anyone else to have to walk with him.

Besides, he was fine with being single. The rodeo life was a good life, even if the thrill of it had grown decidedly thin in the past few years. Maybe next year he'd see about having some kind of a home base. He didn't mind washing his own socks, but he sure did miss a steady drawer to put them in.

Still, rodeo riding was what he knew and what he was good at. No one expected anything from him in the rodeo world that he did not know exactly how to give them. That should be enough for any man, he told himself as he reached Jenny's door.

Zach stamped his feet lightly outside the door, shaking the snow off them. He wore his heavy coat over the Santa suit and carried the mistletoe in one hand and his duffel bag in the other.

"What the...?" Zach muttered to himself as the mistletoe pricked him. The spikes on the holiday weed were big enough that the whole thing should be declared a lethal weapon. Zach half hung the mistletoe on his coat pocket and reached for the doorknob before he hesitated.

Polite manners were never his strong suit. But he

figured even if the light in the window was for him, he was still company in this house and would be expected to knock rather than just come inside as though he belonged here. No matter how tempted he was to do just that, it wasn't right. He didn't belong. So he knocked.

The window on the door was frosted over, but the light from inside shone through the iced pattern.

"Come in," Jenny called softly from inside the kitchen.

Jenny had decided payment of a debt required some special touches. She brought down two cups and saucers from her good china set. She'd even put a lace cloth on the folding table. That should be enough, Jenny thought to herself when she heard Zach on the porch. The tea and the check should bring them about even.

When he opened the door, however, Jenny decided she should have forgotten the tea and left the check until the morning. She should have done whatever was necessary to be as far away from this man as was possible in her old house. The cold had turned the man into someone who looked as if he belonged on one of those calendars for single women. He was Mr. December.

Jenny shivered all the way down her spine. She told herself it was because of the cold wind that blew into the kitchen in the quick second before Zach turned to close the door.

But it wasn't.

Just look at him, she thought in dismay. Zach was the kind of man she had moved a thousand miles to avoid. Montana men were supposed to be farmers. Steady, reliable men with faces one learned to love. She wasn't supposed to meet a man like Zach, whose face would make a nun shiver. But there he stood against the black of the night like some mountain man covered with snow.

The kitchen was dark except for the half dozen candles Jenny had lit, some on the counter and some on the table in the middle of the kitchen. The candlelight made the snow scattered over Zach's dark hair glisten like confetti. The cold had turned his skin to marble. His brown eyes simmered beneath strong brows, and snow had settled on his eyebrows. More snow had fallen on the shoulders of his heavy leather coat as it hung from his frame.

In that long coat, all hints of a friendly Santa were covered.

"Thanks for waiting up," Zach said as he stood on the rug by the kitchen door and set his duffel on the floor nearby. "It was nice of you."

Jenny was speechless. Then she decided the best way to deal with the situation was to meet it rationally.

"It was only for a few minutes." Jenny took a deep breath and walked closer to him as he tried to get his arm out of his coat. If she could only get that coat off him, she'd be fine. She could cope with a man dressed as Santa. "Here, let me help you with that."

Zach stopped in surprise. He couldn't remember the last time anyone had offered to help him with anything. He'd always had to fend for himself. "I can get it."

"Not with that Santa suit on under your coat. Believe me, I know. Andy has a playsuit out of that fuzzy material and it's almost impossible for one person to get the coat pulled off the sleeves."

"Oh."

Zach was pretty sure Jenny was wrong, but he hoped she didn't discover the fact. She had moved close enough so he could inhale the pure soap smell of her.

Jenny gripped the edge of Zach's coat sleeve and tugged.

"Something's caught." Jenny pulled on the sleeve again before looking up at Zach.

Jenny looked back down at the sleeve. Looking up was a mistake. She needed to keep focused on the Santa material. Polyester. That wasn't sexy. Think of Andy's playsuit. "It'll come off in a minute."

Zach wasn't paying any attention to her words. He wondered if she knew what the candlelight did to her blond hair. She'd combed the short curls back and had them clipped with some combs. But little wisps of hair escaped here and there making it look as if she wore a halo.

Zach caught his breath. His skin was still cold from outside, but Jenny slipped her hand inside the sleeve of his coat and his skin warmed up in a hurry.

"Andy's coat never did this." Jenny bit her lip as she frowned up at Zach.

"Huh?" Zach stopped breathing as her hands slid farther under the Santa suit and up his forearm. Her hands were soft as an angel's beneath the weight of both the Santa suit and his sheepskin coat.

"Ouch!" Jenny said.

"Ouch!" Zach said.

The ball of mistletoe dropped to the floor and rolled.

"Sorry. I forgot I'd hung that halfway in my pocket."

"It's mistletoe."

Zach noticed Jenny didn't sound any too happy about the fact.

"It was on the truck antenna. Delores put it there," Zach said.

Jenny nodded curtly. Delores was a matchmaker. She'd put mistletoe on a hearse just in case the corpse met anyone on the way to his own funeral.

"I couldn't just leave the stuff outside. It'd freeze." Zach bent down and gingerly picked the mistletoe up by the string that had tied it to the antenna. "Besides it is a Christmas decoration. Thought you might be able to use it."

"I guess we could put it in the laundry room," Jenny offered after a moment. After all, Delores did mean well. "With the ham."

"What's a ham need with a wad of mistletoe like ours?"

"Ours?" Jenny looked up at him quizzically. The shadows in the kitchen left her eyes in darkness. Zach wished he could see them more clearly. Her eyes gave away her emotions, and he felt that he was flying blind when he couldn't see them.

"Well, you know—you and the kids," Zach stammered, before he added himself to the list. Man, that woman made him nervous. "You don't need to worry about it being mistletoe. I mean with the kissing and all. It's not like I'm planning to kiss you."

Jenny blinked. She wasn't planning to kiss him, either. Of course not. "Good…that's good."

It was good they understood each other. Very good. She would have had to speak to him if he intended to kiss her and assure him that they had no prospects. That would have been awkward, and she was glad there was no need to do it. But still…

"Not that I don't want to kiss you." Zach threw that in for good measure. Jenny still wasn't smiling. "Any man would want to kiss you. I mean you're very, ah, pleasant. Very pleasant."

Jenny frowned slightly. *Pleasant* sounded like someone's grandmother. No wonder he was stuttering and stammering all over himself. Apparently she wouldn't have had to speak to him at all. "You don't want to kiss me."

"Huh?"

"Not that it's a problem," Jenny chattered. When she was upset, she always talked too much. "Which is for the best. Of course. In fact, you shouldn't even think about it. I mean, there's no need—I mean, well, you're just snowed in for Christmas. Stranded, really. We're not even each other's type—I mean, it's not like we're—that is—you just brought the mail and I'm grateful for that.''

Sometimes a man has to gamble with his life, Zach thought. Sometimes he even has to gamble with his heart.

Zach bent down and kissed Jenny.

Or at least he thought he did. Maybe she was the one who tilted her head back and arched up to meet his lips. He would never know. All he knew was that he was kissing Jenny.

Zach had never expected the rush of pure sweetness to be followed by a hint of fire. That was his only excuse for lingering over the kiss.

Jenny stood rooted to the floor. She knew it was a mistake to kiss this cowboy, knew it when she'd told herself to step back and then found herself unable to do it. What was wrong with her, anyway? She usually had more sense. Something was wrong with her. It was—

''Christmas,'' Jenny whispered the word to herself as if it was a lifeline. Of course. It must be because of the holiday that she was letting this man kiss her senseless. That was it. The holiday.

People did strange things at holidays. They ate fruitcake. Rang old metal bells. They even forgot their very sensible vows and kissed good-looking cowboys who were just passing through.

"Hmm." Zach smoothed back Jenny's hair. "What about Christmas?"

"It's making me crazy." Jenny tried to collect herself. What was that purring in the back of her mind? "Well, not just me—both of us—Christmas and mistletoe. You know, it's crazy."

Zach didn't like this line of thought. "Christmas doesn't make people go crazy."

Kisses like the one we'd just shared might make people go crazy, Zach conceded to himself, but a date on the calendar never would. He'd missed out on a lot of things about Christmas, but crazy wasn't one of them.

"Of course it does." Jenny stepped farther back and kept chatting. Even her teeth were nervous around this man. She was lucky she wasn't blabbing. "There's the Santa fantasy. Every kid gets carried away with Santa. Even when we're adults we expect magic at Christmas."

"You think us kissing is about Christmas?"

Zach's voice was quiet, but Jenny didn't stop. She couldn't stop.

"Well, you know the goodwill, peace toward men—that kind of thing."

"I see." Zach turned slightly and, even with one hand holding the mistletoe string, pulled his arm away from his coat sleeve. A slight buzz of static filled the silence.

So that's why Jenny kissed him—goodwill? A man certainly couldn't go very far with that. A woman kissed her uncle for goodwill, or a child. She probably got extra points for cozying up to a sick orphan.

"It didn't mean anything. The kiss, I mean," Jenny stammered. The man was scowling about something. She supposed it was the kiss. He was experiencing after-kiss remorse. She'd seen it before. "We were just—"

"I know—" Zach hung his coat on one of the hooks and tried to stop scowling "—crazy at Christmas."

"Yeah."

Zach could vouch for the fact that at least one of them was crazy. The bottom had sure fallen out of his stability. And people wondered why he wasn't overly fond of the holiday.

Jenny shook herself. "It was only a kiss." And a tidal wave is only a little water, she mocked herself. She felt as if she'd jumped into the deep end before she'd learned to swim. She'd never meant to be this vulnerable again. And him, he was only passing through on his way to— "You were just lonesome for your friend."

"Huh?"

"The showgirl."

"Oh, Cathy."

"I thought you said her name was Patti."

Zach didn't like the way Jenny was looking at him—as though he was such a roving cowboy that he didn't even remember names. "It is Patti. I just call her Cathy sometimes."

Now she'd think he was certifiable, for sure. Zach assured himself the only reason he couldn't remember names was because Jenny was making him nervous. Usually he did fine.

Jenny continued chatting. "Speaking of your trip…" She willed herself to stop, but it did no good. She didn't even like to think about his trip to Las Vegas. She surely didn't want to talk about it. "You'll be needing some money."

"What?" Did she think he was paying for it? "Patti's a showgirl, but she's not—I mean, she doesn't charge."

Zach wondered if she thought he was so unattractive he needed to pay for it. She'd already made it clear she didn't particularly like his looks. But to say that—well, it was pretty discouraging when he'd just kissed her.

"I meant for gas. You'll need to buy gas to get there." Jenny willed her mind to focus. There she'd gone and insulted his girlfriend. And him, she supposed. "All I mean to say is that I have a check for you."

"Gas money?" Zach repeated in disbelief. He wondered if the woman knew how much money he had in his bank account. When he compared it with what was probably in hers, he was speechless. He could buy her miserable little farm a dozen times over and still have change. "I don't need gas money."

"Well, you'll need something someday—and you've done so much for us tonight." Jenny made the mistake of looking up directly into Zach's eyes. She'd heard of eyes that smoldered, but she'd never actually seen any that did until now. He was angry. The gold in his eyes sparked until it melted the brown. She completely forgot what she was going to say.

"You don't owe me anything."

"Still." Jenny gathered herself together. She needed to be strong for her children. She walked over to the counter and picked up the check. "I don't want to be beholden."

Zach saw the cornered pride in Jenny's eyes. So that was it. His face softened. "You're not beholden. You've offered me shelter in a storm. That's worth more than some ride in the dark."

"But it's just an old sofa."

"I've slept on worse. Many nights."

Jenny held out the check. "I'd still feel better if you took this."

Zach didn't want to take her check. Of course, it probably didn't make any difference since he'd never cash it. "I guess."

Zach reached out to take the check with one hand. The other hand held tight to the mistletoe string.

The kitchen was quiet except for the tick of the battery-operated clock on the wall. The candles carved out pockets of golden light by the counters and the table in the middle of the room.

Zach heard a shuffle in the corner and a yawn. Come to think of it, he'd heard the shuffle for some time now. He wondered how long the little feet had been standing there.

"Mama, it's too late to give Santa a letter." Andy's voice came from the doorway to the kitchen. "Mr. Lightning already took the letters to Santa Claus, didn't you?"

Andy padded over to Zach and wrapped his arms around one of Zach's thighs. "You're cold."

Zach was surprised the cold didn't stop Andy from hugging his leg. "It was cold out there—going to the North Pole."

Zach let his hand rest on the boy's head.

"You should be in bed," Jenny gently scolded. Jenny didn't like the fact that her son had gone to the cowboy instead of her for the third time tonight.

"But Santa won't get your letter," Andy said worriedly as he looked up at his mother. He didn't leave his post by Zach's leg as he pointed to the check Zach held in his hand.

"That wasn't a letter. It was a check." Jenny hoped her son's fascination with the cowboy didn't turn to tears when the man left.

"Santa doesn't need a check."

"No, the check was for Mr. Lucas." Jenny hoped the formal title would remind Zach that just because her son wrapped himself around his leg at every opportunity he got it did not mean they were anything but strangers.

"It should have been a list," Andy protested. "What you want from Santa."

"Santa doesn't come to mommies," Jenny said.

Andy's eyes grew wide. "Because they've been bad?"

Jenny smiled. "No, it's just that Santa is special for little kids."

"But won't you get any presents?" Andy was frowning as he clutched Zach's leg even harder. "You've gotta have a present."

"Of course she'll have a present." Zach frantically thought about what else might be in his duffel bag that could be made into a present for Jenny. No wonder Santa was fat. The stress of thinking of all those Christmas gifts would drive anyone to eating too many cookies. "I just don't know what yet."

"We could give her the Christmas ball," Andy announced as he pointed to the mistletoe that hung from Zach's other hand. "I've seen those. They're for kisses. Mommy likes kisses."

"She does?" Zach watched the pink sweep across Jenny's face. "Now isn't that nice."

Andy nodded happily. "I kiss her every night and she sleeps with my kiss under her pillow."

"She does?"

Andy nodded as he pretended to scoop a kiss out of the air. "I blow one to her so she can catch it."

"Isn't that nice." Zach wasn't at all in favor of that kind of kissing. Not when it came to Jenny. Of course, the pillow part sounded nice.

Andy squeezed Zach's leg tighter. "Is Mommy going to keep your kiss under her pillow tonight?"

Zach heard Jenny's gasp.

"Mommy, ah…" Zach jumped in to explain before Jenny could deny everything. He knelt down so he was facing Andy directly. "Your mommy only has room under her pillow for kisses from her little boy. You give her special kisses."

Andy nodded happily. "I blow them to her."

Zach nodded. "That makes them easier for her to catch."

Andy leaned closer to Zach and whispered into his right ear. "I could teach you how to make special kisses. Then you could blow some to Mommy, too."

Jenny didn't like seeing the two heads together. Plus she couldn't hear what her son was saying. She didn't want to spoil Andy's illusions about the cowboy, but she didn't like him sharing his innocent thoughts with the man. "What's the secret?"

"Nothing." Zach knew Jenny wouldn't like what her son was saying.

Her son has no such hesitation. "I was just telling Mr. Lightning how to give you kisses that you keep under your pillow."

Jenny blushed.

"You should be back in bed," Jenny reminded her son. "It's cold out here."

"Tomorrow night Santa comes," Andy said blissfully as he continued to hug Zach's leg. "We're going to make cookies for Santa tomorrow, aren't we?"

Zach wondered when he'd become such a sucker

for little boys. Maybe it was when they offered to teach him how to kiss their mothers. "Sure enough."

"I can stir," Andy offered proudly.

"You'll do a fine job," Jenny said firmly. "But first, you need to go to bed and sleep."

Andy yawned as he let go of Zach's leg and walked back out of the kitchen. "Good night, Mr. Lightning."

"Good night."

Zach watched Andy go. Now there was a sweet little boy, full of hope and enthusiasm. "His father must have been something."

"What?" Jenny looked up at Zach in alarm. Now where had that come from? She never talked about her husband. She'd not even told Delores about Stephen. At first, she'd never told anyone about Stephen because she kept intending to talk to him first. But then he was sick. And now she felt it was disloyal to voice her disappointment about someone who was dead. "What about Stephen?"

"To have raised a boy like Andy, he must have been a good father is all."

Zach was surprised at the surge of envy he felt. It must have felt good to be a man like Stephen and have something steady and loving to give to a wife and kids.

Jenny bit her lip. "Stephen wasn't well."

"I heard...the cancer." Zach could have kicked himself. Jenny's face had gone closed and pale. What kind of a brute was he, bringing back painful memories. "I'm sorry. You must miss him."

Jenny nodded. That was the sore truth of it. Even though he had kept to himself, she missed him. She had loved Stephen. For years. He had been her chosen one. She'd been hopeful. She'd prayed. She'd bargained for his attention. She'd lived expecting the day would come when Stephen would look around himself and realize the value of his family. That day had never come. She always felt there had been some trigger in Stephen that she hadn't been able to find. Something she should have known that eluded her.

Zach called himself ten kinds of a fool. "I should be telling you about my trip to the frozen north instead of stirring up sad memories—especially at Christmas."

"And I should be offering you a cup of tea." Jenny gestured to the table. "And thanking you for making this Christmas a better one for my children."

Zach tried not to notice that she didn't include herself. "The Santa stuff was all Delores's idea."

"Do you like your tea plain or with lemon?" Jenny walked back to the fondue pot. "I'm afraid it will only be a tea bag in a cup. I couldn't get enough water to heat to make a pot."

"A cup will be more than fine."

Jenny poured him a cup of tea in silence and took it to the table. "I'm sure you'll enjoy some peace and quiet while you drink this."

Zach could have told her that he'd lived his life

with peace and quiet. It wasn't what it was cracked up to be. But he didn't. She was rattled. He hoped she'd sit down at the table with him and have a cup of tea, as well.

"The tea smells good," Zach offered. "If you don't have enough water for two cups, I could get by with a half cup."

There. He'd asked her to share.

Jenny shook her head. "It's cold out there. You'll need your whole cup. Besides, I think I'm going to head to bed."

Zach watched Jenny walk out of the kitchen. "Good night."

Zach told himself he shouldn't mind. He was, after all, used to sitting at a table by himself and eating. It shouldn't even bother him after all those years. He'd sat alone in coffee shops. In hotel rooms. In bars. He should be used to it.

Zach looked around at the shadows in the empty kitchen. Yeah, he should be used to it by now.

Suddenly he had no appetite for the tea.

Chapter Six

Jenny woke with her pillow twisted around her shoulders. She'd had a dream of hot coals hiding under her pillow, and it took a couple of deep breaths to assure herself that everything was all right. She could feel her cheeks were aflame even though the air around them was cool.

She was lying on the mattress in her bedroom of the old house in Montana. The faint light of daybreak streaked into the room through the gap between her drapes. The day looked subdued. It was probably cloudy outside. Most likely the electricity was still off. At least the wind had died down.

Jenny heard the quiet giggling before she even had a chance to turn over again. She couldn't mistake the sound of Andy's laughter, and it didn't take too many guesses to place the deeper tones. Zach.

Jenny wondered what she was going to do with her son. How did you tell a four-year-old that it wasn't wise to become attached to a man who was going to be gone in a couple of days?

Maybe you didn't, Jenny said to herself as she stood up and slipped on her robe. Maybe all she could do was distract Andy as much as possible so that he was busy with other things and stopped spending time with the cowboy.

Jenny looked at her face in the mirror on the back of her bedroom door and grimaced. Her blond hair was naturally curly, and this morning it was flyaway. Usually her hair was only like this when it was going to rain. She wasn't sure if her hair would react the same way to snow.

Fortunately, no one would notice her hair once they got a good look at her puffy eyes. She looked like someone who had been doing battle all night with her dreams. Too bad she was out of eyedrops.

She was a mess. But she wasn't in a beauty contest today. All that mattered today was getting Christmas ready for her children. She, like her son, would do well to forget the cowboy was even here.

"Whoever gets the pan out of the cupboard gets the first pancake," Jenny announced firmly as she stepped into the living room.

Three pairs of eyes turned to her. She hadn't realized Lisa had joined the other two. Her two children were in their pajamas. The cowboy had at least put a shirt on with his well-worn jeans. The three of them were huddled around something on the living room floor.

"Mama!" Lisa squeaked.

"Don't look," Andy added in panic.

The cowboy simply pulled a blanket off the sofa where he had slept and spread it over something on the floor. "It's okay now."

Jenny eyed the blanket-covered lump on the floor. "What's that?"

"Well, now," the cowboy drawled. "That depends."

My goodness, Jenny thought as she looked at him closer. Didn't the man ever have a bad day? He looked just as pleased with himself as the children did. And his excitement made his brown eyes—well, it wouldn't do to look him in the eye for too long. "Depends on what?"

"Whether or not I tell you depends on whether you can keep a secret."

"She can't keep the secret. It's—" Lisa protested before she bit off her words and looked at Zach with reproach. "You're teasing."

Zach grinned back at Lisa. "Sure am."

Lisa smiled back before she rolled her eyes.

Jenny felt the need to sit down. Lisa never took to strangers. Granted, she'd run off to the North Pole with the man, but that was only to win a bet. Now Lisa was talking to him as if he was her best friend. Jenny wasn't sure she liked it. "You've got a secret?"

"Don't you know you're not supposed to ask questions at Christmas?" Zach finally said as he stood up.

Jenny was momentarily distracted. She thought rodeo cowboys were supposed to have aches and pains in every joint. Zach moved with a smoothness that made her mouth grow dry. If he ached anywhere it was unnoticeable. His whole body was a symphony. Even his hair behaved. And that little dimple she sometimes glimpsed on his chin—Jenny stopped herself.

"Huh?" Jenny looked away from the cowboy and back at her children. They were sitting on the floor and both smiling at her.

"Oh, it's a Christmas something? For me?" Jenny finally understood. Now she was completely dumbfounded. Jenny couldn't remember the last time she had gotten a real present. She'd always bought herself some soap or bath gel and put "From Stephen" on the package at Christmas. When the children asked, she'd told them all she wanted was a kiss and a smile.

"It's a surprise," Andy said in satisfaction as he stood up and walked over to her. "From us."

"You'll like it," Lisa added confidently as she stood up. "But you can't see it. Not until you open it up on Christmas morning. We're going to put it under the Christmas tree."

"I wouldn't dream of peeking," Jenny said. She hadn't seen her children so excited for months. And Zach—the man stood square in the middle of their excitement, looking just as pleased as they were.

Well, almost as pleased. The dimple was hidden, and she could see a small frown starting on his forehead.

"Where'd you say that frying pan is?" Zach asked as he sat down on the sofa.

"Me first," Andy squealed as he ran out of the living room with Lisa following close behind him.

"I hope you don't mind us doing this," Zach said quietly to Jenny. "Andy woke up first, and we didn't want to wake you. It was early. So we had this idea of making a present. I didn't think to ask you. Maybe, as I think about it now, I should have gone in and woken you."

No, Zach said to himself, that wouldn't have been a good idea at all. The sight of Jenny all warm and curled up in her bed would not have been—well, it would not have been a good idea at all.

"Ah, no." Jenny felt her cheeks blush. She'd already had hot coals under her pillow this morning. "You don't need to ask permission. But Andy can be a handful."

"He's just excited. Christmas, you know."

Jenny knew Christmas wasn't what was exciting Andy. It was having a grown man sit on the floor and pay attention to him.

"He's a good boy," Zach offered. He didn't want Jenny to think he minded spending time with Andy.

Zach had always liked children, but most of his encounters with kids were short and came about because the kid wanted his autograph or wanted to pet

Thunder or something like that. He'd never had a chance to spend this much time with individual children like Andy and Lisa. He hadn't known what he was missing.

"I just don't want you to feel you need to spend all of your time fussing with the children. I know you don't like all the stuff that goes with holidays."

"I don't mind the children." What did she think he was? A monster? "It's only the holiday that I said that about—just the day on the calendar. Never the children. Children are supposed to like holidays."

"Oh." Jenny tried again. "Still, if you have other things to do—reading or something."

"The only books here are the children's books."

Jenny shrugged. "I thought maybe you brought something to read."

"I guess I could go check out the mailbag and see if I forgot to deliver any letters to Mrs. Goussley," Zach teased. What did she think? That he hauled around a library in his duffel bag?

Jenny gave up. Stephen had always found some excuse to avoid spending time with the children. She figured she had given Zach enough excuses he could pick one up anytime he wanted. She'd given him all the help she could.

"Unless—" Zach finally figured out what was giving the woman heartburn "—unless you'd rather I not spend time with the kids."

"What?"

"I know some women think that a rodeo man

might not know how to act around kids," Zach said, ignoring the fact that even he knew he didn't know how to act around kids. "But I've been watching my language. And I don't tell them anything that they shouldn't know about."

Zach almost mentioned that he hadn't even explained what a showgirl was when they asked again this morning. He'd let them keep thinking a showgirl was nothing more than a cheerleader with feathers in her hair. Zach stopped himself from speaking of the showgirl, however. Jenny didn't seem to approve of showgirls.

Instead Zach decided he'd list his good points.

"I might not be as well mannered as their father... and educated," Zach continued. She could stop him at any time, but she didn't seem inclined to do so. "And I'm sure they still miss him something fierce. But, one thing I can guarantee, and that is you can trust your kids with me."

Jenny was speechless. Zach wanted to spend time with her children.

"They're not perfect children." Jenny felt she should let him know. "Lisa bites her nails."

Zach nodded. "I noticed. But I thought maybe she'd grow out of it. It's not something to worry about, is it?"

"I asked Delores about it. She said maybe it's just the move."

Zach nodded. "I'm sure moving around is hard on kids."

Moving around is hard on everyone, Jenny thought, but didn't say it. Maybe she should have stayed in Los Angeles. At least in Los Angeles she would never have gotten stranded miles away from the nearest neighbor with a man who cared about whether or not Lisa bit her nails.

"Mommy!" The call came from the kitchen.

"Oh, the pancakes," Jenny said. "I better get going."

"Take your time," Zach said as he turned toward where he'd laid his coat. "I need to get those pipes put back together before you can cook anything, anyway."

"Oh, I forgot."

"Now that it's light, it'll only take a few minutes." Zach walked out of the living room and into the kitchen.

Jenny stood up. "In that case, I'll dress first."

"Wear something warm," Zach called back from the kitchen. "We need to get that tree in before it starts to snow again. I told Lisa I think I know where we'll find one."

Jenny nodded. How was she supposed to protect her children's hearts from this man when he promised them a Christmas tree in the middle of a Montana blizzard?

Jenny wore panty hose under her jeans and two flannel shirts over a T-shirt. She figured that should keep her warm enough outside. She figured wrong.

The pancakes had fried up nice and brown and

she'd even been able to warm the maple syrup. Everyone had eaten their fill. They had barely pushed their chairs back from the table before Lisa asked if it was time to go to get the tree.

"I don't see why not," Zach said. He didn't like the looks of the heavy gray clouds outside.

"There's the dishes," Jenny reminded everyone.

Lisa and Andy groaned.

"It's going to snow later," Zach said. "Maybe we should go right away."

Lisa and Andy looked at Zach and beamed.

"Well, maybe just this once we can do the dishes after we get back," Jenny conceded.

"You can put them to soak," Andy offered. Soaking the dishes was Andy's favorite way to cope with them. Lisa, on the other hand, carefully scrubbed each dish with a sponge.

"I'll at least clear the table while everyone gets dressed," Jenny said to her children. "And remember double socks today."

"Don't you have anything warmer than those shirts?" Zach asked when the children had left the kitchen.

It wasn't until this morning that Zach figured out that the men's flannel shirts Jenny was wearing had to be left from her husband's wardrobe. No wonder the woman wouldn't let them go. If they were real flannel, they'd probably keep her comfortable in the cold. But they were the thin, city flannel that was set for style instead of weather.

"What's wrong with these shirts?"

"Nothing. They're just not warm enough."

Jenny lifted her chin. "They'll have to do."

"You could borrow a sweatshirt from me," Zach offered and then held his breath. "I've got a new one—not even worn—picked it up at a rodeo in Fargo a couple of weeks ago."

"What makes you think it's warmer than my shirts?"

"Those are California shirts. Made for the beach. The sweatshirt was made for North Dakota wear."

"I wouldn't want to impose."

"And I wouldn't want you to catch your death of cold." Zach thought he had the upper hand, but he decided to cinch it. "Who will take care of your kids if you come down with pneumonia?"

"I won't get sick," Jenny assured him. She couldn't afford to get sick.

"Then you'll wear the sweatshirt," Zach ordered. "And the sheepskin coat."

"Oh, I can't possibly—I can't wear your coat," Jenny sputtered. She needed to draw the line somewhere. She was used to taking care of herself. It wouldn't be good to let down her guard and become used to someone doing things for her. She'd have to cope on her own again when he was gone. Besides, she'd always been a fair person. "You will get just as cold as me. It's your coat. You'll need it."

"I can't wear it, anyway, while I chop down the tree." Zach only hoped they found a tree to chop down. He'd look foolish chopping down a thistle bush. "You might as well wear it. If not, it'll just stay sitting on the seat behind me."

Jenny looked at the coat. Maybe she could let her guard down a little. It was Christmas, after all. And the coat was lined with a heavy knotted wool. "That's not real sheepskin, is it?"

Zach grinned. "Imitation."

Jenny walked over and touched the coat. The rough, knobby lining was warm.

"Try it on."

Zach held the sleeves to the coat as Jenny slipped her arms into it.

"Feels like fur," Jenny said. The coat made her feel warm for the first time in days. She almost felt like purring.

"Now you're ready to go." Zach looked at Jenny with satisfaction. She finally looked like a Montana woman.

Lisa was the first one to spot a tree. After Zach had scraped the ice off of the front and side windows, the four of them had squeezed into the postal truck and driven down the road that ran along the fence of the Collins property.

Just like Zach remembered from the previous day, the only trees around were at the bottom of the coulee about a half mile past the fence, just as the road turned up the hill to go to the house.

Zach had to give Lisa credit. She had leaned over

her mother's shoulder so she could look out the side window. Since Lisa had already insisted Jenny roll down the window on their side, that meant Lisa's nose was cold enough to be red.

"I see one. I see one. I see one. Stop right here." Lisa bounced on her feet as she stood on the floor of the postal truck and half leaned out the passenger-side window.

"We need to pick one that doesn't have any pine-cones," Jenny announced as she pulled out a narrow, green book from a bag she carried. She started to flip through the pages. "And, it's also good to find one that's at least—" she turned a page "—eight, maybe even nine feet tall."

Lisa seemed familiar with her mother's green book. The girl didn't even look at the book, she just nodded dutifully. "We will, Mama."

"What's that?" Zach eyed the book that Jenny read. He had assumed the bag held cookies or crackers in case the kids got hungry.

"It's my Montana Guide Book. It's got a chapter on caring for local trees." Jenny lifted her chin. Jenny had ordered the book when she first discovered that Stephen had not sold his uncle's property. The guidebook had given her the courage to move north. "I don't know very much about Montana. But the people who wrote this book do. They say there's no excuse for just stripping the land of its trees. A good farmer doesn't do that."

"We're only talking one tree," Zach reminded her

as he turned the ignition off on the postal truck. He'd already pulled the truck to the side of the road in an area between two snowdrifts. "That's hardly stripping your land."

Jenny tightened her grip on the green book. "The trees with pinecones are needed to make seeds for new tall trees."

"Well, there is that." Zach nodded.

He didn't have the heart to tell her that it would take more than a few pinecones to make nine-foot pine trees grow on her land. The trees at the bottom of the coulee were hunched over from the wind. He doubted any of them would ever grow more than four feet tall. And those were the lucky ones. Any tree seed unfortunate enough to fall on the top sides of the coulee would never live to grow even to four feet. The wind would see to that.

"I want a tree with an angel hook," Lisa announced as she sat back down on the floor at the back of the postal truck and pulled on her mittens.

"That's just something they put on trees at the lot where we got them in L.A., dear," Jenny said as she sat her book down on the tray that ran along the front of the postal cab. "These trees won't have them."

"Will they have one of those kissie-toe things?" Andy asked as he crawled up front and held out a mittenless hand to his mother.

"You mean mistletoe?" Jenny asked hesitantly. She had hoped Andy had forgotten about the kiss he'd seen last night. She put her hand in the pocket of

Andy's coat and pulled out his missing mitten. "No, the tree won't have that."

"Then how is Mr. Lightning going to learn how to kiss?" Andy forgot about his mitten and just stood in the space between Jenny and Zach.

Zach felt a little hand clamp on to his arm and looked over to the boy. Andy's eyes were earnest with worry as they looked back at him. Zach would have joked with the boy, but he looked over the little one's head and saw Jenny. Joking might not be the best idea, Zach decided.

"Mr. Lightning doesn't need to learn how to kiss," Jenny finally said firmly as she reached around the truck's gearshift to capture Andy's bare hand. Jenny pulled the mitten on Andy's hand. "Now, be sure you have your coats buttoned up tight before you go outside."

Zach held back his grin until his muscles ached. He could watch Jenny's face blush a hundred times and not grow tired of the wonder of it.

"I'm zipped," Andy said happily as he wiggled back into the back of the postal truck.

"Me, too," Lisa said as she unhooked the back door of the postal truck.

"And wait at the edge of the coulee. We'll all walk down together," Jenny called out as the two children scrambled out of the back of the truck. "I need to talk to Mr. Lucas for a minute first."

Jenny wished she didn't blush. "I'm sorry. Sometimes kids say the craziest things."

"I suppose it's because of Christmas." Zach agreed solemnly. It occurred to him he hadn't been able to get a clear picture of Jenny's eyes last night when they had kissed. The candlelight didn't give off enough light. "I hear everyone's crazy at Christmas."

"Yes, yes, that must be it." Jenny was relieved he seemed to understand. "They just get excited, and… well, they don't mean anything by it."

"I must say, though, it is a little troubling." Zach turned so that he was looking squarely at Jenny.

"What is?" Jenny turned to face Zach.

Zach reached up to touch Jenny's cheek. It was cool and smooth as silk. "How can I let your son think I don't know how to kiss his mother?"

"He's talking about air kisses," Jenny whispered. She felt the man's thumb as he rubbed it down her cheek. Her cheek was cold, and his thumb felt like a hot brand, marking her cheek as his own. "The kind you blow across the room."

"Seems an awfully risky way to send a kiss," Zach said softly as he moved closer. "And not nearly as satisfying."

Jenny swallowed. Or at least she tried to—she was having a hard time even breathing. "We need to go get the tree."

Zach must have kissed over a thousand women. Never once in all those times had he wanted a signal as desperately as he wanted one from Jenny. He didn't want to kiss her unless he knew she wanted him to kiss her.

"Is that what you want?" There, he thought to himself, he'd just put the question out there. He didn't want to have any doubts. "The kids are warm. They can wait a minute."

"No, I don't want to...yes, I mean...the kids—" Jenny stumbled. She needed to remember the kids. She was going to find a steady, stable man to be a father to her kids. She couldn't afford to be sweet-talked by a cowboy who was just passing through. "The kids want a tree."

Zach swallowed. Never let it be said he took rejection badly. He was a grown man. He knew the odds. He put his hand on the door handle of the truck and pushed. "Well then, let's go get us a tree."

The tree was deformed. But Lisa had chosen it, and Zach had dutifully cut it, and they had all dragged it up out of the coulee.

"It's got a place for stars," Lisa said as she patted one of the branches.

They had set the tree up in the middle of the living room. Jenny had produced a plastic bucket, and they had poured rocks around the tree trunk to make it stay upright. Even with the extra height of the bucket, however, the tree didn't top four feet. It also had a tendency to tilt to the left.

"It's beautiful," Jenny declared loyally.

"It's crooked," Lisa confessed, a worried frown on her face.

"Some of the most beautiful things are crooked."

Zach anchored the tree deeper into the bucket of rocks. "Remember that leaning tower in Italy."

"Yeah." Lisa smiled. "We'll just have an Italian tree."

Jenny had taken Delores's camera with them and she'd taken a picture of Lisa, Andy and Zach as they all measured that tree down at the bottom of the coulee. And then she'd taken a couple more of them dragging the tree up out of the coulee. "And I'm sure we'll think of something for decorations."

"We don't have decorations?" Lisa stopped studying the tree and turned to her mother. It was clear all worry about the tilting of the tree was forgotten. "We have to have decorations."

"We can make decorations," Jenny said firmly. She should have shown her children how to make decorations in the years past. It's just that Stephen never liked the mess that projects like that made and so it was easier to just buy things at the thrift stores.

"But how can we make stars?" Lisa said worriedly. "Stars need to sparkle."

Zach sat down on the sofa to get a better look at the tree. He didn't know whether he was coming or going. He'd looked ahead down the road on the way back from getting the tree just to see if he could make it into Deep Gulch. He could tell it would be foolish to leave this house, especially because the clouds had started to grow gray and heavy again.

Of course, no matter how foolish it would be to leave, staying would be worse.

Life had really pulled a fast one on him. Here he was, snowed in with a family that was everything like the family on that Christmas card he'd seen when he was ten. Everyone cared about each other. They didn't need a tree to be happy together, but they had a tree anyway.

They made a perfect Christmas card picture. Sure, the father might be missing from the picture, but the man used to be in the picture. For years and years, this Stephen guy had been the husband and father in this family.

The man was dead and buried. And Zach still envied him like he'd never envied anyone in his life. That man had had it all.

"I bet he never rode a horse, though," Zach said aloud to himself.

"Huh?" Jenny looked over at Zach. For the first time today, he looked a little frayed around the edges. Zach was sitting on the sofa with his shoulders hunched forward and his hands clutching an empty cup that had held coffee.

"Horse." Andy caught the one word that interested him. He had been sitting on the floor at Zach's feet. Now he jumped up and stood at Zach's knee. "Are we going to ride a horse? Huh? Are we?"

"We don't have a horse," Jenny answered her son.

"And lights," Lisa moaned. She was still looking at the tree. "We don't have any lights."

"I can take the lights off those reindeer horns on the postal truck," Zach offered as he stood up. He might not be part of this family, but he still wanted this Christmas to be perfect, Italian Christmas tree and all. "They are on some kind of batteries."

Lisa brightened. "That's right."

"And we can make stars out of aluminum foil." Jenny started toward the kitchen. "And I have some red yarn for bows."

"Mr. Lightning has a horse," Andy said softly as he watched Zach walk toward the kitchen door.

"That horse is sick," Lisa said in disgust. "You can't ride a sick horse."

Zach stopped himself from promising the boy a ride. It would be a promise he couldn't keep. Once Thunder was well, they needed to keep driving down to Vegas. He and Thunder were both roving souls. Besides, he doubted Jenny would ever invite him back for a visit. "I'll bring in the reindeer horns. Maybe we can rig you up a horse to ride from them."

"See," Andy said to his sister. "I am going to get to ride."

Lisa just shook her head. "First you have to help make stars."

Zach stepped into the kitchen. Jenny had opened a drawer on the counter and was pulling out slender tubes. "I know I had tinfoil here somewhere."

"I have some foil in the truck."

Jenny looked up, relieved. "You do?"

"Wrapped around half a dozen plates of cookies."

"I could replace the foil with waxed paper," Jenny offered. "That way your cookies won't dry out."

"I thought I'd bring them in anyway. The kids will like them."

"Oh, we couldn't take your cookies."

"They're not my cookies. They were meant for Delores. She'd want the kids to have them."

Why was it, Zach asked himself, that it was so difficult to give that woman anything? Even a porcupine had fewer prickles.

"Well, thank you." Jenny pushed the empty tube of foil back into the drawer. Why was it that the man insisted on being so nice? Couldn't he see that she was determined not to let him get under her skin? "I'll pay you for them, of course."

Zach just looked at her as he grabbed his coat off the hook. What was it with this woman? "I don't need your money."

Jenny was going to point out that everyone needed money, but the man was out of the door before she could. Still, she had made her point. She wanted to keep things on a businesslike level between them. Money helped do that. She didn't like accepting things from him. It made her feel as if they were friends.

No, she admitted to herself, it didn't make her feel as if they were friends. Friends stayed around. They didn't leave and take your heart with them. No, the last thing Zach offered was friendship. At the moment he was a stranger, just passing through, and she would do well to remember it.

Chapter Seven

Zach had a towel wrapped around his fingers and a hot sheet of metal in his hand. It wasn't the best time to be watching Jenny as she watched the sky. He wondered if she knew her blond curls shone with golden highlights as she stood in the thin light that came through the window above the kitchen sink. And the long curve of her neck as she looked up— well, as Zach already knew, it wasn't the best of times for him to be holding a hot sheet of metal.

He'd already burned himself once today when Jenny bent over to pick up a spoon that fell on the floor. Of course, it had almost been worth it when Jenny insisted on rubbing some kind of an ointment on his thumb. She'd been shy about touching him, and Zach had found it more arousing than any flirtation he'd ever encountered.

"Expecting geese?" Zach carefully set the cookie sheet on the pot holders Jenny had laid out on the counter. The kitchen was warm and the sounds of the children in the living room made him feel a contentment he'd never known. For one brief day he was inside the Christmas picture.

Andy had gone into the living room to fold tinfoil stars with Lisa. Jenny had been doing dishes, until she stopped to look up at the sky.

Jenny turned toward him. "It's below zero out there. There's no geese."

Zach nodded. "I know, but the way you've been watching that sky I figured you must be watching for something."

"I was looking at the clouds." Jenny had resisted the temptation to bring her green Montana Guide Book out from her bedroom. Before starting the dishes, she'd carefully read the different cloud descriptions. If she could just match the clouds outside with the right picture in her guidebook, she should be able to tell if it would snow more today. Unless there was more snow, Zach might leave. She didn't want that to happen—for Andy's sake, she told herself. Gray and heavy clouds meant snow. The clouds outside were gray, but she wasn't sure if they were heavy enough.

"Ah." Zach started lifting the cookies off the pan and onto a platter.

"What makes air heavy?"

Jenny hardly recognized the cowboy. He had flour

on his face and a sprinkling of cinnamon on his shirt. He'd tied an old dish towel around his waist. If the cereal people could only see him now, they'd take a whole new set of pictures for the backs of their boxes.

"Moisture, I guess." Zach carefully nudged the angel cookies to the left of the platter so there would be room for a few sugar-cookie trees. He'd never thought he would ever be baking Christmas cookies. "Don't tell me you're worried, too. I thought Andy was the only one."

"Andy's worried?" Jenny didn't like that her son was worried about whether or not it would snow. Of course, Zach had probably mentioned the roads to Andy. "Have you said something to make him worry you'd leave?"

"Me, no. He's not worried about me. He's worried about Santa Claus. Andy's afraid that if it rains instead of snows Santa won't be able to land his sled on the roof because it'll be too slippery." Zach kept his tone light. "It seems he remembers when you tried to fix the roof."

"Oh."

"Something about the roof being slippery because it was raining." Zach took a deep breath so his panic wouldn't show. He knew it was none of his business what this woman had decided to do last month. But what if she had fallen off the roof instead of just sliding down the roof a bit? He wouldn't have even been there to get her to the doctor. "I guess that guidebook of yours didn't tell you that you shouldn't be climbing around on a roof in the rain. Especially not a pitched roof like this one. It's dangerous.''

"Well, I didn't know the roof leaked until it started to rain.''

"That's what buckets are for.'' Zach put the empty cookie sheet back on top of the stove. He had one more pan in the oven. "You wait until the roof is dry to work on it. Besides, you shouldn't be fixing your roof, anyway.'' Zach bent his head down to open the oven and mumbled the rest. "I'll see it gets done for you.''

Jenny didn't think she had heard him right. "But you can't do it, either. Snow's no better than rain. Well, it has to be worse—snow is wet and ice both at the same time. Besides...'' Jenny didn't finish. They both knew he would be gone before the snow melted.

Zach swallowed. The hot air from inside the oven felt good on his face. He reached in for the pan of snowman cookies. He might as well say this while he was facing the oven. He didn't expect Jenny would like it. But he had given it some thought. "I've decided—when I go back to the doc's—I'm going to give him money to hire someone to put a new roof on this house.''

Jenny gasped. She forgot all about the dishrag in her hand. "But, you can't. Why, that's way too much...you can't possibly.''

Zach pulled the pan of cookies out of the oven and straightened up. "Consider it a Christmas present.''

Jenny dropped the dishrag back into the dish water. "That's not a Christmas present—a Christmas present is socks or a pin—something small. A roof is way bigger than a Christmas present." The warm air from the oven floated across the kitchen toward her. "Besides, you don't even like Christmas."

"Maybe not, but I like solid roofs."

"But you can't pay to have a new roof put on my house. Why, what would the doctor and Delores think?"

"They'd think you were getting a new roof."

No, Jenny thought to herself, they'd think she was getting a new husband. Which was ridiculous, of course. Anyone could see the cowboy wasn't the kind of guy to marry anyone. He would never settle down. He'd just—no, Jenny realized with a start, the doctor and Delores wouldn't think of marriage at all.

She'd been out of the dating game for so long, she didn't recognize the obvious. They wouldn't think the cowboy was doing any favors, they'd think she'd been the one to be generous to the cowboy. Anyone would think that. Even Zach. "I could never accept a gift that expensive. It'd be hundreds of dollars."

Try thousands, Zach thought. But he wouldn't sleep well nights thinking Jenny might be crawling around up on that roof. And paying someone to do it was the only way. Unless... "If you won't let me pay someone, I'll come back and put a new roof up myself."

Jenny looked at him as if he'd offered to burn her

house down instead of seeing that it stayed dry. "I have the children to think of, you know. Not to mention the fact that I have to live in this community." Jenny paused. "I'm afraid you wouldn't get anything in exchange for the roof."

"I wouldn't—" Zach had been scooping the cookies off of the sheet and turned too fast. The back of his hand hit the hot sheet. He barely felt the burn. He'd figured out what Jenny was saying and he didn't like it. Not that he wouldn't have tried to find an angle with any other woman he found attractive. "*I* can think of the children, too, you know. And I wasn't expecting anything in return for the roof."

Jenny had noticed his wince when his hand hit the sheet. She reached in her pocket for the tube of ointment. "Then why were you offering it?" She held out her hand. "Here, let me see your hand."

Zach held out his closed fist. The ointment felt cool until Jenny rubbed it around on the back of his hand. Then his whole body heated up. "Can't someone do something nice for you just because—" Zach scrambled for a reason "—just because it's Christmas."

"You're doing it because of Christmas? You?" Jenny obviously wasn't convinced.

Sometimes, Zach decided, a man needed to stay with the cards he'd been dealt, even if they were losing cards. "I have a lot of Christmas presents to make up for. From the past."

"I didn't know you in the past." Jenny held Zach's burned hand while she reached over to the counter and picked up the roll of gauze she'd used on Zach's thumb earlier. She started to unroll the gauze. "You don't owe me any presents."

Zach closed his eyes. Why did she have to make it so hard? "Maybe I've decided it would be too difficult to track down everyone I've known over the years and give them a belated present."

Jenny wrapped gauze around Zach's hand. "So this roof—it's like penance for all your past missed gifts."

"Something like that." Zach closed his eyes wearily. He hoped she never discovered that just because he didn't believe in Christmas didn't mean he'd been stingy in the past.

Ever since Zach had started making good money on the rodeo circuit, he'd given some very nice presents to people. Of course, they were usually checks. Some of them, however, had even been for dollar amounts that would be more than Jenny's roof would take. Never, however, had Zach had as much trouble with anyone accepting a present as he was having with Jenny.

"And you're not expecting to sleep with me in return?" Jenny asked the question crisply. She was just making sure they understood each other.

Zach opened his eyes at that. "Lady, you won't even kiss me. I'm not fool enough to think a roof would get us to where you're thinking."

Zach hoped she'd protest. Hoped she'd say it might at least get him a date. She didn't.

Instead Jenny slowly knotted the gauze on his

hand. She didn't even raise her eyes to his but kept her eyes on his burn. "But I don't have anything nearly that expensive to give you in return."

Zach smiled. So it was her pride that was bothering her. He turned his bandaged hand so that he held hers. "At the rate I'm going, maybe you should just give me that ointment in your pocket and a roll of that gauze."

Jenny looked up and smiled back, but she didn't remove her hand. "Cookie baking can be dangerous."

"I never knew kitchen duty could be so hazardous." Zach couldn't control his thumb as it rubbed the back of Jenny's hand.

Jenny had been washing dishes and her hands were still slightly damp from the water. Even damp, Zach wagered they were smoother than other women's hands.

Jenny's cheeks were pink as she smiled. "If you think this is exciting, wait until tomorrow.. You can help me with the ham. And—if you really want a thrill—you can help open the can of yams I'm going to bake."

"It can't be any harder than baking these cookies." Zach settled back into holding Jenny's hand.

Zach couldn't remember ever holding a woman's hand before. He couldn't remember even wanting to hold a woman's hand. He was always too intent on winning a bigger prize. What a fool he'd been, he thought as he squeezed Jenny's hand. He hadn't known what he was missing. He would remember this moment forever.

The warm smell of sugar cookies made the kitchen cozy. Jenny had rolled the dough thin, and Lisa and Andy had used cookie cutters to shape snowmen, angels, bells and trees. Zach had measured the ingredients and helped Andy stir. Everyone had sprinkled colored sugar on the different shapes before Zach slipped the cookie sheets into the oven.

The sky outside was gray, and only a thin light shone through the windows. The electricity was still off but Jenny had lit a candle and set it on the folding table. The glow of the candle cast yellow light all around the kitchen.

Jenny held her breath. She couldn't remember ever having someone sit with her at the end of a day and hold her hand. It should feel innocent, even with the hypnotic feel of Zach's thumb as it traced circles on the back of her hand. But it didn't feel the least bit innocent. It was one of the most erotic moments she'd ever experienced.

Too bad erotic was a mistake.

"Thanks for helping with everything," Jenny finally said to Zach as she gently removed her hand. "It'll be a wonderful Christmas."

Jenny looked around her kitchen with satisfaction. For the first time, she didn't notice all the things she didn't have. Instead she saw that the folding table still had scraps of tinfoil from the star shapes that Lisa had cut earlier and the kitchen counter was covered with every platter she owned. Each platter was covered with Christmas sugar cookies.

Such a wonderful Christmas merited a wonderful present for the man who had helped make it all possible.

"I can think of a better gift for you than a first-aid kit," Jenny said firmly. She was full of goodwill. Everyone inside her home would have a good Christmas if it was in her power to give them one.

The light coming in from the kitchen window cast shadows around Zach's eyes. "I'm not expecting anything. You don't need to— I mean, the roof doesn't require a present. It's just because—"

"No, I need a present for you." Jenny closed her eyes. How could a cowboy in worn jeans and a towel apron covered with cookie dough look so sexy? Well, it wasn't his fault she couldn't keep her eyes off him. He'd been good to her children and she owed him a Christmas present. She did a mental review of the boxes in her bedroom. "Maybe something of Stephen's—"

"No." The word sounded abrupt even to Zach's ears. Jenny's eyes flew open. To hide his confusion, Zach turned and stole a warm cookie from a platter. "I mean, you should save his things for Andy and Lisa. When they're older they'll want some things to remember him by."

Jenny wondered if her children would remember their father in twenty years. If they did, it wouldn't be because of some sweater or tie.

"He must have been a wonderful father and husband." Zach tried to sound casual as he took a bite out of the cookie.

Zach hated himself for trying to find out more about the man, but the man's very existence bothered him like a scab that wasn't healing right. Maybe someone would let something slip, and Zach could learn the secret that this Stephen had known about being part of a family like this one.

Maybe—Zach didn't dare even hope—but maybe the secret was something Zach could learn if he only had a few pointers. Zach almost choked on the rest of what he had to say, but he said it anyway. "I wish I could have known him. What was he like?"

"Like?" Jenny's voice squeaked. She never talked about Stephen. He was not only a closed chapter in her life, she'd buried the book, as well.

"Yeah. Did he have any hobbies?" Zach supposed the man liked opera. Women always seemed to like opera. Zach preferred a guitar player in a bar anyday. Still, he supposed he could learn to endure opera. "Anything you and he did for special evenings?"

Jenny tried hard to think. She and Stephen hadn't done anything social even in the years before he was sick. Stephen preferred to go out with his male friends rather than stay home with her, and he never wanted to spend the money for a baby-sitter so they could go out together. "We didn't have a lot of money."

"I see." Zach figured that meant they spent a lot of cozy evenings at home putting together jigsaw puzzles and watching videos. The very thought of it depressed him.

Zach would have had a better chance of competing if Jenny had mentioned dinners in fancy restaurants and dancing. He could afford to fly her to Paris for a weekend. It was the home things he wasn't sure he'd ever get right.

The outside light was fading in the kitchen, and the glow of the candle on the table was growing more golden. Zach's face picked up the glow of the candle. He was concentrating on the cookie in his hand with an intensity that reminded Jenny of his picture on the back of that cereal box.

It was the cereal-box picture that gave Jenny the courage to decide to tell Zach the truth about Stephen. She wanted to tell someone. She really did. The words always just seemed to stick in her throat. But if she pretended she was talking to the back of that box, maybe she could get the words out.

"Stephen—" Jenny began and swallowed. She felt almost relieved now that she had decided to tell someone. Even if that someone was just a cowboy who was on the back of a cereal box. "Stephen was, well, it wasn't so much what he was, it's what he— Well, you know I've told you that he wasn't—" Jenny stopped. Zach had turned and was looking at her. All of a sudden, he didn't look anything like his picture on the cereal box.

"Yeah," Zach prompted her.

"I, ah…" Jenny knew it was her chance. She also knew she was a coward. She didn't know what Zach would think of her if she told him about Stephen. Lots of men thought any marital unhappiness was the wife's fault. Maybe Zach would think that, too. "I... we got married awfully young."

Zach almost groaned. No wonder Jenny didn't want to kiss another man. Stephen was probably the only man she'd ever even dated. "You must have been very much in love."

"Uh..." Jenny swallowed. She would try again.

Jenny never got a chance. The quiet giggles from the living room had grown louder and finally they were at the kitchen door.

"Mama, come look," Lisa called as she stood in the doorway.

The house was in shadows.

"Oh, I better get the lantern lit," Jenny said. She'd talk to Zach later. It wasn't that she wouldn't have talked to him, she assured herself. It just wasn't the time yet. She'd tell him all about Stephen. And soon. Just not right this minute. She couldn't risk the children hearing about Stephen.

"Mr. Lightning," Andy called from the living room. "Come see the stars."

Zach followed Jenny into the living room, and the light from the lantern she was carrying made the tinfoil stars reflect a thousand lights. The tree glowed with the reflections. Zach had unwrapped the Christmas lights from around the reindeer horns that Delores Norris had hung on the postal-truck hood. He'd then clipped the lights to the branches of the Christmas tree. The battery for the lights was nestled on top of the rocks at the bottom of the tree. So far, no one had turned on the lights.

"They're lovely," Jenny said as she put one hand on Lisa's shoulder and smiled at Andy. "I've never seen so many stars."

"Can we turn the lights on now?" Lisa asked. "It's almost dark."

Jenny had told the children earlier that they would turn on the tree lights when it grew dark. Jenny wasn't sure how much power the batteries had left, and she didn't want to run the batteries dry before it even grew dark.

"Let's have some soup first." Jenny looked at her watch. How had the day gone so fast. "It's almost five o'clock. Then we can read the Christmas story before you go off to bed."

"But that will still be too early," Lisa protested. "I wanted to wrap your present."

Zach had hidden the jewelry box the kids had made for their mother earlier this morning. The jewelry box had really been a small wooden toolbox that Zach had kept his leather-working tools inside. Andy had glued some beach shells he'd found in California on top of the box and Lisa had glued a piece of velvet on the inside of the box.

Wrapping presents, Jenny thought in dismay. "But I don't have any paper. Oh, I knew I wasn't ready for Christmas."

"Wrapping paper isn't necessary," Zach said, hoping he was right.

He was wrong.

"Yes, it is," Lisa said, and she looked up at Zach like he was a magician with a hat that still had a few miracles left inside of it.

"I don't have any—oh, wait." Zach remembered. "I do have paper. In the postal truck. Delores carries around a tube of brown postal paper. And tape."

"Brown paper?" Lisa looked skeptical.

"I think there might be some red stamps and some markers." Zach wasn't sure what all Delores kept in her postal bin that ran along the right-top side of the truck.

"We can make Christmas paper," Jenny said in relief. The kids would remember Christmas paper they had made themselves a lot longer than anything she could buy.

"Just remember, you need to go to bed early tonight," Jenny said firmly. "Remember what we said? If you go to bed early, you can get up early tomorrow morning."

And, if they go to bed early, Jenny added to herself, she and Zach would have time to make the presents for the children they'd talked about earlier. Zach had told her his ideas, and she knew the children would love the gifts he had suggested.

"All right," Lisa agreed reluctantly.

"Can I have cereal instead of soup for supper?" Andy asked.

Andy had also asked to have Ranger cereal for lunch when the rest of them had eaten tuna sandwiches. Jenny had given in then. "You've got to eat more than cereal."

"I can have a cookie, too," Andy offered.

Jenny appealed to Zach. "You talk to him."

Zach smiled. He was glad the cereal executives couldn't hear him now. "Real cowboys don't eat cereal for every meal. They need other things, too, to stay healthy. Maybe you should try some soup tonight.''

''Are you eating soup?'' Andy asked as he walked over and wrapped his arms around Zach's leg.

''I sure am.''

''Okay,'' Andy agreed. ''I'll have soup. And crackers?''

''Yeah, we have crackers. And peaches for dessert.'' Jenny tried to remember everything she had in the cupboards. She was grateful Stephen's uncle had had the good sense to see that the kitchen stove operated off the propane tank like the furnace did. With the electricity still out, they wouldn't be eating anything warm if he hadn't.

Zach left his hand resting on Andy's head. Zach liked the solid weight of the boy as Andy leaned against his leg. ''Let's go set the table for your mom.''

''I know where the bowls are,'' Lisa announced as she led the way.

Supper was by candlelight, and Zach was content. He'd eaten candlelight dinners in five-star restaurants at the top of skyscrapers and on cruise ships. At none of those dinners had the conversation lagged or the soup been cold. But he didn't even have to debate the issue. He wouldn't trade this candlelight meal for any one of the others.

''At least the peaches should be all right,'' Jenny said quietly.

''It was a wonderful meal,'' Zach assured her. ''Wholesome.''

"I could heat up some more tomato soup, now that the stove has cooled down." Jenny hadn't realized that using the oven of the stove all afternoon would affect the burners. It meant they wouldn't stay lit for very long.

"I'm content."

Jenny wondered if she should admit to Zach that she was content, too. She wondered at the ease she felt around him. Earlier in the day Jenny had realized she was relaxing around Zach because he didn't criticize her the way she had expected any man would. Zach seemed to be pleased with whatever she had to offer in the way of meals and household comforts.

Zach was a big change from her late husband. Stephen had been visibly unhappy if the laundry wasn't ironed right or the meals weren't to his liking. No wonder she'd been tired all those years when she'd been married, Jenny thought to herself in amazement. She'd been trying to make things perfect for Stephen. And perfection had been hard to maintain when she had two small children to care for as well.

Of course, Jenny told herself, it was easy for Zach to accept things the way they were. He wouldn't be around long and he probably just didn't care.

"I do know how to cook a good meal," she added in self-defense. "It's just the stove and all. I'm learning."

"We're all learning." Zach pushed his chair away from the table. "Let me get the peaches for you."

"After peaches, I want to make wrapping paper," Lisa said.

Jenny rinsed the dishes from supper and left them

in the sink. Amazing how liberating that felt. For the second time today she hadn't needed to rush to do the dishes as if she had something to prove to someone. Instead the four of them sat at the folding table and made wrapping paper.

Andy liked to stamp. He'd stamped a red FRAGILE over a length of brown postal paper. The stamp was upside down in some places and sideways in others. Jenny noticed that the confused jumble of it all did manage to look festive.

Lisa was drawing bells with a red pen on another length of brown postal paper.

"I'll need to remember to pay Delores for all this," Jenny said.

"I bet she'd like a picture instead," Zach said as he stood up and walked to the kitchen counter. If he knew anything about Delores, he knew she had a soft spot for these two children. The woman deserved to see them as they concentrated on decorating the postal paper.

"Great idea," Jenny said as she accepted the camera Zach handed to her.

Jenny snapped two pictures and pulled them out to dry. She'd taken a dozen or so pictures of the children over the day. There was one of Andy and Zach cutting out cookies. There was one of Lisa and Zach stringing the lights on the Christmas tree.

Each picture Jenny took, she took two shots. One of the shots was for herself. The other one was for a Christmas present for Zach. She'd thought about going through the box of Stephen's ties and sweaters.

But, even though Zach wouldn't be wearing either

one around Jenny, she didn't like to picture him in anything but the clothes he already had. She didn't want to look at the cowboy and see any reminders of Stephen.

Actually, she thought she might take the whole box of Stephen's things and tie it up tight with some of Delores's postal string before setting it at the back of the large closet in her bedroom. Zach was right. Andy and Lisa might want to see the things someday, but for now, Jenny wanted it tucked away where she didn't have to see it every day.

Jenny couldn't help but wonder, as she listened to her children giggle while they talked with Zach, what her life would have been like if she had married a man like Zach instead of one like Stephen.

Well—she shook herself—that was a pointless thing to wonder about, and on a Christmas Eve.

Chapter Eight

Zach had never heard the Christmas story read to children. Oh, he knew the story. The star. The wise men. The shepherds. The angels. The baby in the manger. But he'd never seen it through the eyes of children.

Zach sat backward on a folding chair with his arms resting on the back. He loved watching Jenny as she sat on the sofa with one child on either side of her and read them the Christmas story.

"And that's why we have peace and goodwill to all on Christmas," Jenny said as she closed the children's book. "Because the baby Jesus was born a long time ago in Bethlehem."

Jenny had moved the lantern into the living room, and it was hanging from a hook she'd rigged up from the ceiling fan. The lantern gave off a yellowish light that bathed the room in a warm glow. The smell of recently baked cookies still filled the air, mingling with the smell of fresh pine from the tree that sat in the bucket of rocks in the middle of the room. A small present was already wrapped and sitting beneath the decorated tree.

"And stars," Lisa sighed. "That's why we have stars."

"Well, we had stars before Christmas," Jenny said softly. She supposed now wasn't the time for a lesson in astronomy. "But none of them were as special as the Christmas star."

"It was the biggest, bestest star ever," Lisa said in satisfaction.

"My star is big, too," Andy said as he pointed to the tree that stood in the center of the living room. "It's that one."

Andy and Lisa had colored their stars. The folded foil stars had been marked with red highlighters and yellow highlighters. Some had flowers drawn on them. One had a horse. They each had a hole poked in their top for a piece of twine so they could be tied to the tree branches.

The stars made the lopsided pine tree sparkle with reflected light from the red and green lights that were twined around the tree branches.

The star Andy pointed to had to be at least four inches across. It was so big it hung crooked on the tree branch. A yellow stick figure had been drawn on it with a big circle around its head.

Zach thought the stick figure must be an angel and the circle a halo.

"It's a beautiful star," Jenny agreed as she shifted the arm she had around the boy and gave him a quick hug.

Andy wiggled down from the sofa and walked over to Zach's chair. "Did you see my star?"

"I sure did," Zach assured the boy. "I think it's the best ever. And that's some angel you drew."

Zach could see Lisa roll her eyes from where she still sat on the sofa. "It's not an angel. It's you."

The girl might as well have thrown a thunderbolt at him. "Me? An angel?"

"It's a cowboy," Lisa said as she stood up and walked over to the tree. She touched the star and then looked at Zach. "See. There's the hat."

"You put me on your star?" Zach repeated stupidly as he looked down at Andy.

The boy was smiling. "I put Thunder, too—on the other one."

Andy went over and touched the star with the horse on it before turning to Zach. "Do you like them?"

"They're the best ever," Zach said as he cleared his throat and then blinked. A bit of smoke from the lantern must have got in his eye. "What a wonderful Christmas surprise."

Andy looked at Lisa and they both giggled.

"That's not your Christmas surprise," Lisa finally said. "We've got that planned for tomorrow morning."

Zach hadn't had the breath knocked out of him this completely since he had been bucked off Black Demon in Fargo last year. He knew his mouth was hanging open, but he couldn't close it.

"We can't tell you what it is," Andy warned. The boy danced in excitement. "It's a surprise."

"Well, I'll be," Zach finally managed to say. "A Christmas surprise for me."

Zach turned to Jenny. He admitted he was a little giddy. Usually the only Christmas gifts he ever got were bottles of booze. "They have a surprise for me."

Jenny had never been prouder of her children. They'd planned a Christmas surprise for a guest in their household without any prompting or guidance from her. Jenny thought about that for a minute, and her pride quickly turned to worry. Her children had planned a Christmas surprise for Zach without her input. That could spell disaster.

Not all men appreciated the same things that children did and Jenny knew that. Granted, Zach had seemed genuinely touched with the stars. But who knew if he'd react as well to some wrinkled tie or cardboard belt buckle.

"I think maybe it's time for bed now," Jenny announced.

Even though both of her children sat with pleased looks on their faces, Jenny was sure one of them would tell her about their planned surprise when she tucked them into bed. If she knew what the big gift was maybe she could straighten a few of the corners or iron it or something. She'd noticed that several of the boxes in the corner of the living room looked as if someone had gone through them this afternoon.

Well, Jenny thought, whatever it was, she would do whatever she could to make it better. If she only knew what it was. Unfortunately, neither one of her children would budge, insisting it was a Christmas-morning surprise and surprises were secrets.

"Well, at least show me before you show it to him. Okay?" Jenny pulled the covers up to Lisa's chin and reminded herself to have her scissors and glue handy in the morning. Maybe she should also get out a needle and thread. "Is the surprise made out of cloth or paper?"

"Mom." Lisa rolled her eyes. "It's a surprise."

"I know, sweetie." Jenny bent down and kissed her daughter on the forehead. "I know."

Zach was in the kitchen, sitting at the table and stamping PRIORITY on a full yard of brown postal paper. He added a few green snowflakes drawn with one marker that still had ink in it. He decided right then that he needed to start carrying a bigger duffel. Either that or he'd have to tell Delores she needed to carry more supplies in her postal bin. He wished he had glitter or velvet or even a red stamp that gave a holiday greeting instead of a postal message. And that was just the stuff at the bottom of his wish list.

Right now, he wished for a whole lot of things.

Ever since he'd seen that star, he'd wished he had time to go to Denver or Salt Lake or at least Billings to buy Christmas presents for this little family. He'd like to buy a princess doll and a tiara with real diamonds for Lisa. She could sell it when she wanted to go to college someday—and with a mind like hers she'd definitely want to go.

Then he'd buy a horse for Andy. And if a real horse would be too much trouble, he'd buy one of those electronic ones that they used in bars. He'd find one with a gentle setting. And, if he couldn't find one with a gentle setting, he'd buy the boy a carousel with a dozen horses to chose from.

And for Jenny—Zach stopped stamping and smiled—for Jenny he'd buy a full-length mink coat. Fake, of course, if she was bothered by the real thing. But something warm enough to weather the worst Montana storm her guidebook ever dreamed could hit.

He'd also buy her a tractor.

But Zach knew there was no time to travel and no clear roads even if there was time. There was no way to get to the gifts he wanted to buy. So he'd just have to make do with what he had.

"They're in bed," Jenny announced as she stood in the doorway to the kitchen. She had brought the lantern into the kitchen before putting the children to bed and its yellow light formed a circle around the table and Zach. The Christmas-tree lights had given off enough light for her to see Lisa and Andy to bed. Both children had promised to go to sleep quickly.

"They've had a busy day." Zach didn't know when he'd had a better day himself. He'd certainly never had a better day related to Christmas. He stopped stamping the brown paper and raised it up. "Do you think I should stamp this some more?"

"It looks good." Jenny had never seen a man so taken with Christmas. "I brought the wire hanger you wanted. And the strip of old towel."

Zach admired Jenny standing in the doorway. The red and green lights from the living room backed her silhouette, while the yellow light from the lantern played up the blond highlights in her hair. Her face looked dewy smooth and sculpted. Her eyelashes were thick and he didn't think she was even wearing any mascara. The shadows hid her blue eyes, and they looked like an ocean at midnight.

Zach swallowed and forced himself to think of the presents he still had to make. The night promised to be even longer than the watch on his wrist indicated. "Thanks for bringing everything. I'd better get started."

Zach had taken his duffel into the kitchen. He'd found a few minutes during the day to slip into the laundry room and pound belt holes in the strip of leather he was planning to use in Andy's gift. The rest of the work would be quiet, and he could do it while everyone slept.

"You're sure you want to cut this up?" Jenny walked over to the counter where Zach had laid out the leg garter and picked it up. The lantern light made

JANET TRONSTAD   149

the rhinestones sparkle quietly. "This had to be expensive."

The black lace and velvet circle studded with rhinestones looked like something out of a classy department store rather than a vending machine. Jenny counted the stones. Fifteen. "Some of these look real."

"The rubies are." Zach rolled the stamped postal paper up. He'd need the whole table for working. "There's only a couple of them. Of course, they're not high quality."

"And you're cutting this up?" Jenny looked at the garter more closely. Those rubies sure did look genuine. "You can't cut this up—not if they're real."

Jenny frowned. She didn't like the fact that Zach had bought something with actual jewels in it for his girlfriend. A garter was one thing, but jewels! Jewels meant commitment. Maybe Zach's relationship with the showgirl was more serious than he had let on. Of course, he did not owe her any explanations about his relationships with women. Zach and her family were stranded together in a snowstorm. He didn't even want to be here. "I'm sure Patti would want the rubies even if you give them to her after Christmas."

"Ah, well, I don't know when I'll see her now. I mean, she expected me today so—" Zach didn't want to admit to Jenny that he'd lost all appetite for his Vegas vacation.

"Oh, and she won't know what's happened. She'll be worried."

"Not likely."

Jenny felt a little better. "She'll probably see the weather reports about a blizzard here. She'll know your trip might have been interrupted."

"Yeah." Zach didn't want to keep talking about Patti. He knew the showgirl wouldn't worry about him at all. "Do you have that hanger? I think that's the first thing to do—see if I can bend that into a likely shape." Zach looked up at Jenny. "Mind if I use your head to size it?"

"Huh?"

"The tiara." Zach took the metal hanger Jenny handed to him and ran his hands along it. "Good quality."

Jenny sat down at the table.

Zach stood up. This tiara-making business wasn't so bad. He realized he had every excuse in the world to touch Jenny's head. "Lisa's hair is the same color as yours. Very pretty."

"Thank you." Jenny felt warm—too warm for a night like this. It was thirty degrees below zero outside tonight, and she knew for a fact that she kept the furnace thermometer set at sixty-five. She should be shivering from the cool instead of the heat—she barely felt Zach's hands as they circled the top of her head. Of course, it wasn't his hands that were bothering her. It was him. He was six feet of muscle standing behind her chair. She could feel the heat from his body. She wondered if he could feel her heart racing. "It's been quite a day."

"Mmm, hmm." Zach tried to keep his mind on the tiara instead of the fact that Jenny's hair was soft enough to kiss. And thick—her curls would scatter over a pillow like the petals of a sunflower. And to think he used to prefer long hair on his girlfriends.

What was he thinking? Zach pulled his hand back. Jenny wasn't his girlfriend. She wouldn't even kiss him. Well, he didn't think she'd kiss him. He hadn't asked again since this morning. And she was sitting awfully still in this dimly lit kitchen. He put his hand back, this time on her shoulder, and she didn't pull away. That had to be a good sign.

"Women—they say they can always change their minds, don't they?" Zach asked without thinking.

"Huh?" Jenny turned around to look at him. In the shadows her eyes were deep blue and unreadable.

"Ah…Lisa. You're sure she wants a tiara?" Zach could have kicked himself. He rode bucking horses, for Pete's sake. He was always able to ride out the shoot when the bar was pulled back. He never wavered. He never hesitated. Until now.

Jenny turned back. "Yeah, I'm sure. She's talked about it ever since we moved here. I wish I'd known sooner. I could have found one in a store in Los Angeles and brought it with us."

"Yeah."

Zach told himself a responsible, decent Santa would get on with making Christmas gifts and forget about the woman sitting in front of him. "And what have you wanted for Christmas?"

"Me?" Jenny laughed. "I've been working too hard to think about what I want."

"You need someone to help you."

Jenny leaned back into the man's hands. He was giving her a back rub. It felt wonderful. "I've been thinking of getting a dog."

"A dog?" Zach almost lost his rhythm in the back rub. That certainly put him in his place. He was losing his touch.

"Yeah, someone to chase the rabbits out of the garden come spring."

"You're planting a garden!" Zach had driven through this part of Montana last summer when there wasn't a foot of snow on the ground. "You'll need to put down a layer of topsoil first. The wind blew it all off a couple of years ago."

"The guidebook didn't mention anything about topsoil." Jenny frowned as she turned around to look at Zach. "It said I could grow anything."

"Potatoes might grow," Zach offered. He pressed against Jenny's left shoulder. "They don't take much topsoil."

"But I want snap peas and roses. Sort of an English garden. And some tomatoes."

"Oh." Zach moved over to the right shoulder.

Jenny felt as if her shoulders were putty. Warm, melting putty. Zach was massaging them with the palms of his hands.

Then Zach moved his hands to the base of the back of Jenny's neck.

Jenny held back the moan that purred deep in her throat. "How'd you ever get so good at this?" Jenny regretted the question as soon as she asked it. A single man like Zach only learned to give massages for one reason.

"My horse," Zach answered. Now why had Jenny stiffened up like that? There, that was better. "He had a leg injury."

"Ah, good," Jenny sighed.

"He didn't think so."

"No, I don't suppose he would."

The massage left Jenny relaxed and energized both at the same time. "I should help you with the presents."

"We've got time." Zach had never felt this content in all his life. Not when he'd bought his first horse. Not when he'd first won the Pro-Championship title. Not when he'd signed the contract with the Ranger cereal company. Not ever. "I like being here with you."

Jenny heard the words Zach whispered. Suddenly she didn't care that he was a man who was just traveling through. "I like you, too."

"Like as in like, or…?" Zach didn't want to shatter the quiet of the evening by making a false move.

Jenny stood up and turned to face Zach. There was only three inches between them. Then there was two. Then…

Jenny figured some women lived their whole lives and never had a kiss like this one. It curled her toes and made her breath stop in her throat. She would have swooned, but mothers with two young children did not swoon. "I feel faint."

"Hmm." Zach still had the taste of her lips on his tongue. He was reluctant to let go.

"I think—"

"Don't think."

"I think I need to wrap the Christmas presents."

Ah, Christmas. Christmas had given Zach trouble for years. Strangely enough, for the first time he didn't mind so much. "You can stamp while I finish up on the other presents."

Jenny not only stamped enough brown postal paper to wrap the gifts, she drew red bells on them. So what if the bells grew to look a little like hearts. It was Christmas, after all, and Christmas was a time for wishes and dreams.

It was even, she told herself firmly, a time for dreams that had no hope of ever coming true. She knew Zach "Lightning" Lucas was just passing through. She knew he wished he was in Las Vegas. She knew he hated Christmas and was just being kind to her and her children. But, even knowing all that, she couldn't help smiling when he walked into the unheated laundry room and came back with the mistletoe in his hand. "We could use this for decorations on the packages."

"It's a pity to waste it," Jenny said. She watched the slow smile spread across Zach's face as she added. "After all, it is Christmas Eve."

Jenny floated to bed that night. She'd had one magical night. She'd been kissed. She'd been hugged. She'd been listened to by someone who paid attention.

If she had to keep reminding herself that it wouldn't last forever, that is what she would do. After all, once Christmas was gone, winter would be long and cold. Her heart would have time to mend.

Chapter Nine

Could kisses give anyone a hangover?

Jenny sat in her bed and wondered how she could feel so bad on Christmas morning. Well, technically it wasn't morning yet, she comforted herself as she looked out the window in her bedroom. It was deep gray outside. The wind had stopped blowing. She had a good half hour before she had to get up and pretend everything was well with the world.

It was Merry Christmas time. Hugs and Santa time.

Jenny wanted to crawl into a dark pit and stay there until spring. But—she squinted at the illuminated clock by her bed—in nineteen minutes, she would smile. And she would pretend that everything was wonderful, even if she had to crawl to the Christmas tree on her hands and knees. Christmas was a special time of the year for children, and Jenny was deter-

mined to add to her children's cheer and not take
away from it.

It wasn't her children's fault that Jenny had gone
crazy last night and thrown caution to the wind. And
crazy it was. She'd fallen in love with a man who
was only passing through—a man who had not even
meant to end up in her house and would have left if
the snow had not stranded him. He had only been
there to deliver a package, for goodness sake. He was
the mailman. And not even the regular mailman. He
clearly wanted to spend Christmas with a showgirl
instead of a widow and her two young children. What
had she been thinking?

Jenny felt around in the semidarkness for the bottle
of water she kept by her bed. Now, if she only had
an aspirin. Or two. She winced. Make that four.

Zach was miserable. He would never be able to
look at another Christmas card again. Or even a postal
stamp—Fragile, Return to Sender, Priority—they
would all be signals to him to count his shortcomings
in the future.

He was a grown man. He should have known he
would have to pay the price for those kisses last night.
Never before had he so deeply regretted the kind of
man he was. If he had any clue as to how to be a
family man, he would take a nail and permanently
tack that piece of mistletoe to the doorway of this
house. And then he'd beg Jenny to marry him.

But he wasn't good at relationships. He didn't even

know how much he didn't know. And it wasn't fair to Jenny to pretend otherwise. It certainly wasn't fair to the kids.

Sure, Zach admitted, he'd done all right for a day or two. He'd filled in for Stephen who should have been here with them. Anyone could follow a good act for a few minutes. It was like riding on a bronc that had been winded by the previous rider. It wasn't a fair test. And it wouldn't take long for Jenny to realize he was a fake.

Zach didn't relish seeing the disappointment in her eyes. He would have to leave. But before he left he owed them a merry Christmas. He was, for better or for worse, Santa Claus.

Zach was just snapping his white beard into place when he heard the first whisper. It sounded like Andy. The answer that came sounded like Lisa. Zach hurriedly put the Santa hat on his head. He'd already put the rest of the outfit on—even that belt with the lights.

Speaking of lights—Zach reached for the battery switch to turn on the Christmas-tree lights. The tree glowed in the early-morning light, casting red and green shadows all around the living room.

The tree sat in the middle of the living room, and the lights danced on all four walls. Zach's eyes were drawn to the bulletin board that he'd seen earlier. He'd avoided the pictures on the board yesterday, but now—knowing his hours with this family were limited—he went over to look at the pictures.

He had to smile. There was a photo of Andy

dressed as a pumpkin for Halloween. There was Lisa in a frilly white dress and almost no teeth. And the zoo—there must have been four or five pictures of the children at the zoo. Andy by the elephants. Lisa by a giraffe. And the beach—there were so many pictures at the beach. In one of them, Jenny was building a sand castle with Andy. That picture was crooked. Lisa must have snapped it.

Zach wondered how many men's hearts were broken on Christmas morning. He wanted to give so much, and he had so little to give.

"What?" Jenny's voice carried from her bedroom. The children were clearly in with her, and a quiet rumble of whispers followed Jenny's first outburst. Zach couldn't make out any of the words, but he could tell a heated discussion was taking place behind the closed door.

Zach wondered if he was about to get his surprise. It sounded like some surprise. He only hoped the wrapped packages under the tree would be sufficient to repay the children for the amount of convincing they were doing. It sounded like an uphill battle was being fought in there.

He wondered what they were giving him that their mother so clearly disapproved of. It must be something like a knife. Mothers always disapproved of knives—as they should. But that couldn't be it. Jenny wouldn't care if he had a knife.

Maybe—and the thought didn't sit well with him— the children had decided to give him something that had belonged to their father and Jenny couldn't part with it. That made sense. Some favorite shirt or tie. Well, she didn't need to worry about him. He would quietly return anything they gave him that had sentimental value.

The voices went silent and then Zach saw Lisa's head poke out of the partially opened door. She looked around and saw him.

"You need to go sit on the sofa," the girl directed him, before giving a worried look back into the bedroom. "We're almost ready."

Andy came out first and ran across the room to settle on the sofa next to Zach. Zach put his arm around the boy before he looked down at Andy's hair. A tiny white feather was sitting on top of the boy's head.

"Dum-da-dum," Lisa trumpeted as she stood in the open doorway.

What the…? Zach watched Lisa sneeze. She had a dozen tiny white feathers flying around her. They floated around her before settling to the floor.

Zach decided the children must be giving him a chicken for Christmas. A live chicken. That's all it could be with those feathers. But where had they kept a chicken? There was only one shed on the property and it was so rickety the coyotes would have torn it down long ago if there was a chicken inside. And he didn't hear any squawking. Only a tame chicken would lose its feathers without squawking. Oh, no, Zach thought. The chicken must be a pet.

"Dum-da-dum," Lisa repeated as she stepped to the side of the door and waved her arm for someone to come onstage.

What the...? Zach's first thought was that there must be a truckload of chickens inside Jenny's bedroom. Tiny white feathers floated everywhere as Jenny stood in the doorway in her—Zach took a second look and started to grin—Jenny was in a red-and-white cheerleader's outfit.

"It's a showgirl," Andy whispered.

Zach grinned like a fool. "That it is."

"You told them a showgirl was a cheerleader with feathers in her hair," Jenny accused him as she stood in the doorway to the bedroom. She held a pom-pom in each hand and an exasperated smile on her face. "Lisa even sacrificed her goose-down pillow so they'd have feathers."

"It works for me," Zach said. He couldn't take his eyes off Jenny. She stood there daring him to laugh. Her blue eyes glinted with steel. Her hair was sprayed stiff and covered with feathers. She was absolutely amazing.

"We have a cheer," Lisa announced as she motioned Andy to join her. "A Christmas cheer."

Zach saw Jenny close her eyes in resignation.

"One...two...three," Lisa counted off before she added, "Now."

The three voices blended. They spelled out the words. "M-E-R-R-Y C-H-R-I-S-T-M-A-S—Merry Christmas to you!"

Jenny kicked her leg up and shook her pom-poms. Lisa and Andy just screamed.

"Did you like it?" Andy asked eagerly before anyone else had regained their breath.

"I liked it a lot," Zach answered. Even if he lived to be a hundred, he would never receive a better Christmas surprise than this. "It's the best present ever."

"That's not all," Lisa screeched as she ran to the kitchen and came back with the camera. She handed the camera to Zach before rushing back to the doorway. "You get to take a picture of us, too."

Zach's eyes were blurry and his hands shook. But he snapped two pictures all the same. Now it really was the best Christmas gift possible. He had pictures of Jenny and the kids.

Jenny watched as Zach carefully set the pictures aside to develop. Well, he'd been a good sport about it. Lisa and Andy were still trembling with excitement, although she noticed their attention had moved from Zach to the wrapped packages lying under the tree.

"Did Santa come?" Andy finally asked softly.

Zach swallowed. "Well now, let's see."

It was an hour later before Jenny was able to convince everyone they needed to eat some breakfast. Lisa was pirouetting around the living room, dipping and twirling with her tiara. Andy was proudly strutting with the Stetson hat Zach had given him and the cowboy belt.

Jenny, herself, had been dumbfounded. Zach had given her his sheepskin coat. She shouldn't accept it.

Jenny knew he didn't have another coat with him and that, even though he claimed the Santa suit would keep him warm until he could buy another one, she still shouldn't take his coat.

But she couldn't resist.

It wasn't because the coat was warm and she'd realized winter would be much colder than her guidebook had indicated. No, the reason she couldn't refuse was because when she had the coat around her, she felt like Zach was with her. The coat carried the woodsy smell of him. It just plain comforted her. And she had a feeling she would need some comforting even before the day was gone.

"I need to have cereal for breakfast," Andy said after Jenny mentioned the meal. Andy swung his twine rope around. "I want some of the cereal that real cowboys eat."

"I think I can arrange that," Jenny said. Even though the electricity was out, the milk seemed to have stayed fine in the unheated laundry room. If anything, the room was probably colder than a refrigerator would be.

"But I don't know what princesses eat." Lisa stopped pirouetting. Her tiara tilted on her head, but she managed to look regal. "Andy can have cereal, but what will I have?"

"Peas," Zach answered. He was sitting on the sofa telling himself he'd never known a single moment in his life when he had been happier. Watching the kids play. Seeing Jenny wrapped in his coat. It was a perfect moment in time. "Canned peas."

"What?" Lisa looked as him suspiciously. She even walked over to him and leaned on his knee. "You're teasing me."

Zach brushed a feather out of her hair. "You've heard of the princess and the pea."

"But that wasn't breakfast, silly." Lisa giggled and rolled her eyes. "That was for her mattress."

"Is that right?" Zach watched Lisa laugh and shake her head. Another white feather floated to the floor. "You mean she sleeps on her vegetables?"

The sun had come up and was shining in the windows. The lights were still steadily lit on the Christmas tree, but the sunshine from outside dulled their glow.

"No, she doesn't," Lisa protested. "Nobody sleeps on vegetables."

Zach gave an exaggerated shrug. "I don't know. Kings and queens do strange things sometimes. I figure princesses might, as well."

"You could have toast and jam," Jenny offered. "And I could fix you some tea like the English make it with milk in it."

"I could be an English princess," Lisa agreed, and then leaned even more on Zach's knee as she looked at him. "And you can be my servant."

"Me?" Zach lifted his eyebrows and smiled at the girl. "Well, I guess you're right. A princess does need a servant or two. I would be delighted to serve you breakfast, madame."

"Not madame, it's Princess Lisa."

"Indeed it is, Princess Lisa."

Zach decided to serve everyone breakfast. He put a kitchen towel over his arm and a falsetto tone in his voice. He poured from the right and removed from the left. He made the children laugh and Jenny roll her eyes in merriment.

And then, when Zach almost had his back turned, he saw Jenny twist the cereal box around so she wouldn't have to see his picture on the back of the box.

"A problem with the box? I could remove it from the table if you like." Zach could hear the hurt in his own voice. No wonder men didn't like to be vulnerable—especially over breakfast.

"It's not—" Jenny started to explain. "It's not you. It's me."

"How can it be you and not me? It's my picture on the box." He might be hurt but he wasn't brain-dead. No one here owed him anything. Jenny didn't need to spare his feelings. Still, Zach didn't want his heart to bleed in front of the children. Especially not on Christmas day. He forced himself to smile. "Not that it matters. More toast anyone?"

Jenny took a deep breath and closed her eyes. "I used to talk to your picture."

"What?" Zach had picked up the empty toast plate and now he held it suspended.

Jenny opened her eyes. "I used to talk to your picture on the back of the cereal box."

"Really?"

"I was lonely," Jenny said defensively. "People pick up strange habits when they're lonely. I mean it's not like I knew you then."

"Really?" Zach had never thought of anyone talking to his picture before. "Really?"

"It's not that big of a deal. It's only a cereal box."

Zach started to smile. He almost started to whistle. "No problem. Anyone want more toast?"

Learning that someone made a habit of talking to your picture could boost a man's ego, Zach thought to himself all through the rest of the morning. It made twenty games of rope-the-foot possible with a little cowboy, as the boy learned to twirl his rope. It made ten dances with a princess possible, complete with nine bows and one beheading for displeasing the royal one. It even carried Zach through peeling potatoes and basting the Christmas ham.

It wasn't until Christmas dinner was finished that it occurred to Zach that Jenny would have talked to a box of detergent if it had been sitting on her table when she was so desperate. A woman whose beloved husband was sick would talk to anything rather than confess her worries to her husband.

"I'm sure he was a very special man—your Stephen," Zach said. Christmas, after all, was a time to think of others rather than yourself. Zach wanted her to know she could still talk to him. "It must be hard to have your first Christmas without him."

Zach and Jenny were sitting alone at the table. The children had eaten and fled into the living room to play. The blizzard had ended sometime last night and the sunlight coming inside now was so strong and warm that no candles were needed. The frost had melted on the windows. It was the middle of the afternoon.

Jenny took a deep breath. She owed it to Zach to tell him the truth—the whole miserable lot of it. But where did she start? "Stephen and I would have been married for ten years this coming February."

"What date?"

"Huh?"

"The date. What date did you get married?"

"February 14, Valentine's Day, although I don't see—"

Zach's shoulders slumped. He was right. This Stephen had been a charmer. What woman wouldn't want to get married on Valentine's Day? How was another man ever supposed to compete with that? "You must have had some memorable anniversaries."

"Memorable is right." Jenny hadn't realized for two years that the reason Stephen had been so intent that they marry on Valentine's Day was so that he wouldn't have to remember a separate anniversary date. Even with the added help, he hadn't remembered their anniversary for the past five years. "But that's not what I want to say."

"I know you loved him." The kitchen was warm and smelled good. Sunshine streamed into the room, and Zach could hear the children playing in the living room. He wanted to wrap the memory of this moment around him tight so that he could pull it out on some lonely night in the future and remember the time he'd been part of a family.

There was a soft ticking, and it took a minute before Zach realized what it was—he was hearing the clock. The electricity was back on.

Jenny swallowed. "Love is a complicated thing sometimes."

"I'd expect so," Zach lied. He didn't find love complicated at all. Painful, yes. Complicated, no.

"It's not always—" Jenny began, and then paused. The telephone rang.

"Service is back," Zach muttered. He supposed it wasn't fair, but he wouldn't have minded if the electricity stayed off for another week. Especially not if another storm moved in and kept them all stranded together. But he'd known since morning that the snow outside was melting. Sure, the road still had a buildup of snow on it, but he might be able to push his way through in the postal truck this afternoon.

"Hello," Jenny answered the phone. "Oh, hi, Delores. I can't thank you enough for—oh, yes, he's here." Jenny paused, listening. "No, no he hasn't shown up yet. Yes, I'll call you then." Another pause.

''No, no, it was no problem. It was good to have him here. Yes, I'll see you tomorrow then.''

It didn't take a snowdrift to freeze Zach's heart. He already heard a distant roar coming toward the house.

Jenny hung up and looked at Zach. ''Delores sent the county snowplow out to plow our road.''

''I didn't think they'd work on Christmas. Isn't that overtime?''

''Double time, but they had to do it. We have the postal truck, and tomorrow is a mail day.''

Couldn't the mail just wait for a day, Zach thought. Or maybe a week. Even a month would be okay. ''So this is it.''

Jenny nodded. ''You'll have to drive the postal truck back.''

But you can come back then, Jenny thought. There's nothing that says you can't come back. We haven't had nearly enough time to…to what, she asked herself. More time would only add to the heartbreak if he was going to leave anyway.

''I'm going to leave the reindeer horns and the lights,'' Zach said. He could hardly speak. How did a man leave when every atom of his being wanted to stay? ''Delores can pick them up later.''

Jenny nodded. ''She told me how grateful she was you drove for her that last day.''

''No problem.''

Zach willed his legs to move. He could hear the snowplow clearly outside now. There were no more excuses to stay. But he still sat.

"You'll be in Vegas late tomorrow." Jenny twisted a knot in the napkin she held in her hand. Zach had never pretended to be anything other than a cowboy out looking for a good time. Even she knew a widow with two little kids wasn't a good time.

"Yeah," Zach lied. He didn't know where he was going. He didn't care. But he had no appetite anymore for Vegas. A grieving man didn't go to Vegas. He'd rather find a deserted hotel somewhere in the open spaces of Utah and lick his wounds for a few weeks.

A man's boots stomped on the porch before a loud knock came at the kitchen door. "I'm the snowplow man."

There was a moment of silence.

"He'll want a cup of coffee," Jenny finally said as she stood to open the door.

"I'd best say goodbye to the kids." Zach stood, as well. The dream was over.

Chapter Ten

"I hear you were one popular Santa Claus," Delores Norris said as she opened the door to her brother's house for Zach. The warm smell of roasting turkey came floating out into the cold air behind her. "Why, I got calls—"

"Calls?" Zach's heart started to pound. He stopped scraping the snow off his boots and just stood there.

Delores nodded. "Mrs. Goussley left three messages telling me how much the cats missed you already and what a great Santa you were."

"Oh." Zach grunted as he started scraping his boots again. The cats.

Christmas had gotten the best of him again. Next Christmas he wasn't taking any chances. He'd head to a deserted island, maybe someplace off the Alaskan coastline. Or maybe Iceland. No one went to Iceland in the winter.

"And, of course, the candy canes were a hit," the older woman continued as she accepted the bag from Zach that held the Santa costume. "They always are."

Delores was just as Zach had pictured her. She had bouncy gray hair and a mouth that didn't stop chatting. Her bright eyes welcomed him like he belonged.

How was she to know he didn't belong anywhere?

"I suppose Thunder is able to travel," Zach said.

"Well, yes, but you don't want to head out this afternoon. You won't make it to a town with a hotel before dark. Besides, we have a spare room and a whole half a turkey left from dinner. There's nothing like a fresh-turkey sandwich with dressing on the side."

Delores was the picture of hospitality with a red-checked apron hanging over a navy sweatsuit. She had pearl earrings on her ears and tennis shoes on her feet. She was looking at him as if he was a long-lost friend.

Zach forced himself to smile. "Thanks, but I'll be moving on. I might make it into Wyoming before nightfall."

"Well, if you're sure." A tiny frown settled on Delores's forehead. "But I'd like a chance to thank you by giving you a night's stay at least."

"No need to thank me."

"We've got pie, too. Apple and cherry. I've never

known a cowboy to turn down a piece of homemade pie.''

"That's kind of you, but I'd best be moving on.''

"Well, all right then.'' Delores stepped out onto the porch and crossed her arms. "Let me just go park the postal truck in its spot.''

"I can move it if you tell me where it goes.''

"It's easier just to show you,'' Delores said with a wave of her hand as she marched off the porch.

"Your feet will get cold,'' Zach called after her. Oh, well, Zach thought, if she didn't care, who was he to make a big deal out of it.

Zach followed her back to the postal truck.

"Oh, isn't this nice?'' Delores had already opened the door and leaned into the truck. She reached out for the photographs that Zach had laid out on the dash.

Zach winced. He'd taken the pictures out so he could look at them as he bounced along the country roads back into Deep Gulch. "I'll just pack them up. Got my duffel in back, too.''

Delores stepped back, holding all four pictures. She squinted in the sunlight as she tilted the photographs up so she could see them better. "Why, aren't those nice?''

"Yeah.'' Zach swallowed. He didn't know what to say. Not that there was anything to say. A picture was just a picture.

Delores looked closely at each picture. Zach didn't have to see the pictures to know what she saw. A picture of Jenny as his showgirl. A picture of Andy roping Zach's foot. A picture of Zach dancing with Princess Lisa. A picture of Zach and the children dragging the Christmas tree up from the coulee.

"Well," Delores said softly as she lowered the pictures and turned curious eyes toward Zach. "Looks like you had some Christmas."

Zach grunted. "I was just doing what I could to make sure they had a good Christmas."

"I see."

"Anyone would have done the same." Zach held out his hand. He wasn't going anywhere without his pictures. "They're good kids."

"Uh-huh," Delores agreed. She didn't hand over the pictures, though. "I don't think I've ever seen the kids like this—laughing and being silly."

"Well, it's Christmas. You know how kids are at Christmas."

"I suppose." Delores took another hard look at him as she handed him the pictures.

The sun warmed the air considerably, but it was still too cold to stand outside and talk. Zach hoped that encouraged the woman to go back inside. "They're just missing their father."

"The kids?" Delores seemed surprised. "Did they talk about him?"

Zach shuffled. He hadn't meant to get into a conversation about the man. "Well, no, but you gotta figure he was a good father. Good husband, too. They got married on Valentine's Day, you know?"

"No, I didn't know."

Zach knew it was time to go. There was only a couple of hours of daylight left, and he'd like to get closer to the Wyoming border before pulling off the interstate for the night. But his mouth just kept talking.

"Must have been tough when he died," Zach added. What was wrong with him? Then he knew what he wanted to say. He knew the question he wanted to ask someone. "Wonder what made him so special anyway?"

Delores looked him over once again. Zach felt her gaze. But the woman wasn't unkind about it. She was obviously just thinking.

"What makes you think he was special?" Delores finally asked.

"Well…I…" Zach stammered. Of course the man was special. "The kids are such good kids and Jenny, well, Jenny is wonderful."

Delores nodded. "Funny thing, though. Jenny never talks about her late husband."

"Well, no, but…"

"Kids don't, either."

Zach was silent. Come to think of it, the kids didn't talk about their father.

"And did you ever see those pictures she's got hanging on the wall in the living room?"

Zach smiled and nodded. "They liked the zoo."

Delores nodded, too. "Ever wonder why there's no pictures of the father there?"

The silence cracked over Zach's head. Delores was right. There were no pictures of Stephen. "What do you suppose that means?"

Delores shrugged. "I don't know for sure." She looked up at Zach and smiled. "But if I was you I'd go ask Jenny about it before I drove away."

"You think it might not have been—" Zach cleared his throat. "I mean, do you think a man like me could have a chance?"

"I'm not the one you need to ask."

Zach figured there was a silly smile on his face, but he couldn't stop the grin from spreading. "Mind if I borrow the postal truck again? I'll be back in a few hours."

Delores grinned back at him as she handed him the keys. "I don't need it until nine o'clock tomorrow morning."

"Tell Doc I'll pick Thunder up later."

"Don't worry. That old horse of yours will be fine here."

The road back to Jenny's place had just as many bumps as it had the first time Zach had ridden over it. The difference was that this time he grinned a little more at each bump he drove over.

Jenny thought she heard someone drive up to her house, but she wasn't sure. She and the children had been sitting on the sofa with blankets snuggled around them. Jenny had offered to read to them, but they both seemed to just want to sit and be quiet.

"I think someone is here," Jenny said softly as she untangled her arms from the blankets.

"Tell them to go away," Andy muttered. "We don't want nobody."

"This is Montana," Jenny chided her son gently as she stood up. "Neighbors are important and will always be welcome in our house."

"If it's a stranger, you should be careful," Lisa advised glumly. "It's not just snakes you have to watch for around here."

"I'll be careful," Jenny said as she started to walk toward the kitchen. "It's probably just the snowplow guy again."

Jenny had to step around the Christmas tree to get to the kitchen. The batteries had died on the tree lights, and the stars didn't sparkle anymore. Andy's hat sat forgotten beside the tree. Lisa's tiara was next to it.

Christmas this year had been both the best ever and the worst ever for her little family.

The sun had melted most of the frost in the small window of the outside kitchen door. But the afternoon had faded and the light had never been good on that side of the house. She saw a shape, but she could not tell who it was. She squinted, anyway—those shoulders reminded her of—not that it would be him.

Jenny opened the door. What in the world—?

Jenny tried to form a word, but couldn't for a full minute. Then it occurred to her that many things could explain why this particular man was standing on her porch. "Forget something?"

Zach smiled. "I guess I did."

"Let me know where it is and I'll go get it." Jenny knew it was rude to leave someone standing on the porch, but she didn't want her children to know he was here. He'd only break their hearts two minutes later when he left again.

"Well, I don't quite know where it is." Zach tried smiling harder. His smile was often called *charming* by women.

There was no smile in return. "We only have the five rooms."

Zach looked at Jenny. She didn't exactly look welcoming. In fact, she barely looked as if she tolerated his presence. Her eyes were guarded. She wasn't smiling. She hadn't invited him into the house and it was cold outside.

All in all, Zach conceded, it didn't look good. But a man didn't ride wild horses because he believed in taking the safe route. Zach reached up and ran his hands around the side brim of the Stetson hat sitting on his head. It was the same gesture he used when he was ready to start a rodeo ride.

"It's more of a question than anything."

"Oh?"

"When you talked to my face on that cereal box, what did you talk about?"

Jenny could hear Lisa and Andy running toward the kitchen. She didn't have much time. "Is this some market-research question? You think your sponsor would like to know? Maybe they'll find some small demographic niche of women who are crazy enough to talk to cereal boxes.''

The footsteps entered the kitchen.

"Mr. Lightning!"

"Santa!"

Two pairs of feet ran to the door and planted themselves beside Jenny.

"You're back!"

"You came!"

Now this was a better welcome, Zach thought as he looked down at the kids. "Hi, there. Mind if I talk to your mom for a minute?"

"Sure," the two voices answered.

But no feet moved. Three pairs of eyes kept looking at him.

"Alone." Zach swallowed.

"Maybe you could go pick out the books you want me to read for you tonight when it's time," Jenny suggested.

"Okay," Lisa said, and started back to the living room. The girl nudged Andy to follow her.

Zach waited until the children were in the living room. "I'm not asking about the cereal box because I care about marketing. I want to know what you were thinking and feeling. I want to know why you don't have any pictures of Stephen on your bulletin board."

"Stephen?" Jenny paused. This was about Stephen?

"Was it because it was too painful for you to have any pictures of him around?"

"No," Jenny answered. "It's just that we didn't have any pictures. Not ones like that. I mean, we have a couple of formal shots—he needed one for a business thing once. But that was taken at a studio."

"Was the man camera shy?"

"Stephen? No."

"Then why don't you have any pictures?"

Jenny suddenly felt very tired. She'd never complained about Stephen. Never complained about him to anyone. She told herself she was protecting him. But now she wondered if she was only protecting herself.

There was such a long pause Zach wondered if Jenny was ever going to answer him.

"Because he was never with us," Jenny finally admitted. She needed to tell someone the truth about her life. "When we went to the zoo, he went fishing with some buddies of his. When we went to the beach, he went to a ball game with some other friends."

"So he wasn't some kind of superfather?"

"Stephen? No. He was barely a father at all."

Zach was beginning to have hope. Maybe he'd do all right as a father. But there was something even more important he needed to know.

"And as a husband? How was he as a husband?"

Jenny looked up at Zach. She saw longing for the children and for her in his eyes. She had never realized until now that Stephen's disinterest in being a husband only added to his disinterest in being a father. The two weren't separate. A man who would make a good husband to her would also make a good father to the children.

Especially, she thought to herself, if it was this man standing before her. She looked at him carefully. She could see the fears in his eyes. The drawn tension around his lips. All pretense was gone from his face. He was letting her see his insecurities and his longings.

Jenny reached up and caressed Zach's cheek briefly. She needed to let him see her as well. All her fears. Her defeats. Her tiredness. "He never loved me."

Jenny closed her eyes. There, she'd said it aloud. Stephen had never loved her.

A moment passed before Jenny realized her fears had not come true. Telling someone the truth about her and Stephen did not cause a crushing blackness in her heart. Instead, her heart felt lighter than it had in years.

Zach reached up and covered Jenny's hand with his. "He was a fool."

"I really tried to make him care." Jenny let Zach draw her into his arms.

"He didn't deserve you," Zach whispered. "You deserve someone better—someone more like, say, me."

Jenny opened her mouth to speak.

"No, don't answer yet. Hear me out." Zach held

her quietly and talked in her ear. He'd never had such an important moment in his life. Every word counted. "I grew up in a family of loners. But I can learn how to be a good husband and a good father. If you just give me time."

Jenny opened her mouth again to speak.

"No, that's not all. I want you to know I work hard, too. We can build a farm here or we can do something else. Whatever you and the kids want."

Jenny opened her mouth again to speak.

"No, that's not all, either. I—"

Jenny reached up and put her fingers lightly over his mouth. She didn't intend to ever hide the truth from this man again.

"If you don't stop talking, how can I ever say yes?"

Jenny had seen her share of sunrises. But she had never seen anything as full of brilliant hope as Zach's face.

"Yes?" he asked. "I mean, I know you would want to wait a few months to be sure, but yes, sometime. That's good."

Jenny supposed it was too much to have expected her children to really sit and pick out books to read when Zach was around. She saw them peek around the doorway into the kitchen.

"Is Mr. Lightning staying?" Andy whispered.

Lisa just rolled her eyes and lifted the camera up to take a picture.

Jenny closed her eyes when the flash hit. She kept

them closed for the kiss that followed. And for the one after that.

Later that night Zach and Jenny together pinned the picture Lisa had taken on the bulletin board. The picture was a little blurry and tilted sideways. But Jenny knew that, even though they would have many more pictures together over the years, this first picture would always be special.

Epilogue

Zach and Jenny decided that April was a perfect month for a wedding.

Zach had finished the new roof by then, and Jenny had planted the first seeds in her garden. They both had taken time to test their first rush of love and be confident that what they felt for each other was strong enough to last forever.

The four months also gave them time to become part of the community of Deep Gulch. Zach took a job as the relief carrier for Delores and rented a room from the doc. Jenny joined the parents' group at the school and volunteered to staff the refreshment stand for the basketball games.

When the organist started the bridal march at the church, almost everyone in and around Deep Gulch was there to watch the two of them say their vows.

Zach and Jenny had told everyone that wedding gifts weren't needed. But the people of Deep Gulch all brought wrapped packages, anyway. There were pink oblong boxes. White oblong boxes. Gold oblong boxes. Delores was the first to notice that the boxes all looked alike. Since she also held an oblong package in her hand she knew what the presents were— dozens of family photo albums. Everyone knew, by now, that Jenny loved to take pictures of her family.

Not that Jenny looked as though she cared what she received for wedding gifts. Delores decided she'd never seen a more beautiful bride.

Jenny herself was holding Zach's hand so hard she was afraid she'd dent the ring she'd just slipped on his finger.

"You may now kiss the bride," the minister announced.

Jenny didn't even notice the camera flashes as Zach smiled and then bent to kiss her.

*   *   *   *   *

$ Saving Money $ Has Never Been This Easy!

Just fill out and send in this form from any October, November and December 2002 books and we will send you a coupon booklet worth a total savings of $20.00 off future purchases of Harlequin and Silhouette books in 2003.

Yes! It's that easy!

I accept your incredible offer!
Please send me a coupon booklet:

Name (PLEASE PRINT)

Address   Apt. #

City   State/Prov.   Zip/Postal Code

In a typical month, how many
Harlequin and Silhouette novels do you read?

❏ 0-2   ❏ 3+

097KJKDNC7   097KJKDNDP

Please send this form to:
In the U.S.: Harlequin Books, P.O. Box 9071, Buffalo, NY 14269-9071
In Canada: Harlequin Books, P.O. Box 609, Fort Erie, Ontario L2A 5X3

Allow 4-6 weeks for delivery. Limit one coupon booklet per household. Must be postmarked no later than January 15, 2003.

PHQ402

If you enjoyed what you just read,
then we've got an offer you can't resist!

Take 2 bestselling love stories FREE!

Plus get a FREE surprise gift!

Clip this page and mail it to Silhouette Reader Service™

IN U.S.A.	IN CANADA
3010 Walden Ave.	P.O. Box 609
P.O. Box 1867	Fort Erie, Ontario
Buffalo, N.Y. 14240-1867	L2A 5X3

YES! Please send me 2 free Silhouette Romance® novels and my free surprise gift. After receiving them, if I don't wish to receive anymore, I can return the shipping statement marked cancel. If I don't cancel, I will receive 6 brand-new novels every month, before they're available in stores! In the U.S.A., bill me at the bargain price of $3.34 plus 25¢ shipping and handling per book and applicable sales tax, if any*. In Canada, bill me at the bargain price of $3.80 plus 25¢ shipping and handling per book and applicable taxes**. That's the complete price and a savings of at least 10% off the cover prices—what a great deal! I understand that accepting the 2 free books and gift places me under no obligation ever to buy any books. I can always return a shipment and cancel at any time. Even if I never buy another book from Silhouette, the 2 free books and gift are mine to keep forever.

215 SDN DNUM
315 SDN DNUN

Name	(PLEASE PRINT)	
Address	Apt.#	
City	State/Prov.	Zip/Postal Code

* Terms and prices subject to change without notice. Sales tax applicable in N.Y.

** Canadian residents will be charged applicable provincial taxes and GST.
   All orders subject to approval. Offer limited to one per household and not valid to current Silhouette Romance® subscribers.

® are registered trademarks of Harlequin Books S.A., used under license.

SROM02   ©1998 Harlequin Enterprises Limited

Silhouette

SPECIAL EDITION™

&

SILHOUETTE Romance®

present a new series about the proud,
passion-driven dynasty

THE COLTONS

**You loved the California Coltons, now discover
the Coltons of Black Arrow, Oklahoma.
Comanche blood courses through their veins,
but a brand-new birthright awaits them....**

WHITE DOVE'S PROMISE by Stella Bagwell (7/02, SE#1478)

THE COYOTE'S CRY by Jackie Merritt (8/02, SE#1484)

WILLOW IN BLOOM by Victoria Pade (9/02, SE#1490)

THE RAVEN'S ASSIGNMENT by Kasey Michaels (9/02, SR#1613)

**A COLTON FAMILY CHRISTMAS by Judy Christenberry,
Linda Turner and Carolyn Zane (10/02, Silhouette Single Title)**

SKY FULL OF PROMISE by Teresa Southwick (11/02, SR#1624)

THE WOLF'S SURRENDER by Sandra Steffen (12/02, SR#1630)

*Look for these titles
wherever Silhouette books are sold!*

Silhouette®
Where love comes alive™

SILHOUETTE *Romance*

COMING NEXT MONTH

#1630 THE WOLF'S SURRENDER—Sandra Steffen
The Coltons

Kelly Madison had been the bane of the Honorable Grey Colton's existence.
Now the feisty defense attorney was back in town, in his courtroom…and
ready to give birth! Grey helped deliver her baby—and, to his surprise, softened toward the single mom. But would his ambitions drive him up the legal
ladder—or into Kelly's arms?

#1631 LIONHEARTED—Diana Palmer
Long, Tall Texans

Inexperienced debutante Janie Brewster had been chasing successful rancher
Leo Hart for years—but he only saw her as a child. At a friend's suggestion,
she set out to prove herself a bona fide cowgirl. But would her rough-and-
tumble image be enough to win over a sexy, stubborn Hart?

#1632 GUESS WHO'S COMING FOR CHRISTMAS?—Cara Colter

Beth Cavell promised her orphaned nephew snow for Christmas—then handsome Scrooge Riley Keenan appeared and threatened all her plans.
When an unexpected storm forced them to spend the holiday together, Beth
wondered if Riley could grant Jamie's other Christmas wish—a new daddy!

#1633 THE MARQUIS AND THE MOTHER-TO-BE—Valerie Parv
The Carramer Legacy

The Marquis of Merrisand might be royalty, but that didn't mean that he could
claim Carissa Day's lodge as his own! Except that it *was* his, and Carissa was
the victim of a con man. A true gentleman, would Eduard de Marigny open
his home—and his heart—to the pregnant temptress?

#1634 THE BILLIONAIRE BORROWS A BRIDE—Myrna Mackenzie
The Wedding Auction

Wanting no part of romance, Spencer Fairfield hired Kate Ryerson to pose as
his fiancée—after all, Kate supposedly had a fiancé of her own so there would
be no expectations. But his ruse wasn't working the way he'd planned, and
soon Spencer discovered the only man Kate did have in her life—was himself!

#1635 THE DOCTOR'S PREGNANT PROPOSAL—Donna Clayton
The Thunder Clan

Devastatingly handsome Grey Thunder wasn't interested in a real marriage—
but he *was* interested in a pretend one! Marrying the emotionally scarred doctor was the perfect solution to pregnant Lori Young's problems. But could
their tentative yet passionate bond help them face the pain of their pasts?

SRCNM1102